QUESTIONABLE TACTICS

By

GAVIN STONE

Other books by Gavin Stone:

The Unforgiven Spy

(Fiction)

How to Tell if Someone is Lying

(Non-Ficrtion)

Chapter 1

Scott Lomax swung his first punch with the speed of a lightning strike. His huge arm, like a helicopter rotor blade with a lead weight on the end, collided with the face of the first inmate. The merciless blow made a crunch as it snapped the man's jawbone, spinning his victim on the spot and dropping him to the floor. The punch was so hard it split the skin and splashed a line of blood up the magnolia-painted wall. The rest of the inmates had an adrenaline spike as their eyes widened, and they braced themselves, ready to pile in. The second inmate jumped forward with an empty dumbbell bar. Mid-dive, Scott Lomax had thrown one of the metal disc weights, like a Frisbee, right into his nose. A crunch preceded the spray of more blood that squirted from his face before he, too, hit the deck.

The inmates that weren't involved rapidly cleared the gym. Plastic water bottles that were left behind in a rush got knocked over and rolled across the floor. Dumbbells and equipment were discarded in the exodus. Trainers squeaked on the rubbery beige cushion floor. The smell of sweaty bodies filled the air, eyes fixed on Lomax from every part of the room. Florescent lighting from the windowless gym in the center of the prison reflected off the gang member's sweaty skin. Each of them now poised with the slightest of aggressive frowns on display. The clinking of weights had completely stopped, and the gym, which was busy only moments ago, was now almost silent.

The young lad named Nathan, who had fallen victim to the prison gang, was immobilized by fear. Scott had taken a liking to him some time ago. One of his mates was getting slapped around in the dining hall as a show of strength by some of the younger gang members. While half of them were fighting, the other half were taking turns spitting in Nathan's mate's porridge. When they had all finished giving him a beating, Nathan switched his mate's porridge with his own without anybody except Scott noticing. Nathan threw the spit-filled porridge away while his mate ate what he thought was his own and what the gang thought was filled with phlegm. This small unmentioned sacrifice by Nathan was enough for Scott to take a shine to the kid.

It turned out Nathan was, in fact, there to take the blame for something his brother had done. Even with this prison spell, though, it didn't deter Nathan from dreaming. He wanted to be the poster child for his neighborhood. The black kid from the gutter who, despite the odds being against him, got educated and moved onwards and upwards to make something of his life. He wanted to show the world that if he could do it, anybody could.

The skinny little kid with glasses that looked like window panes filling half of his face was terrified of the gang that ruled the prison mercilessly. Today, they'd started to push him around a bit too much. They had dragged him into the gym and were about to ramp things up when Scott had gotten involved. It was only a matter of time before the guards stormed in, but Scott was certain he was going to teach these assholes a lesson before the screws made it to the room. Scott had held back for too long. Today the hammer was going to fall. And when it came to dishing out vengeance, Scott Lomax was a weapon like no other. A nuclear temper with an animal instinct.

Individually none of these guys would have dared to go up against Lomax. Collectively they must have thought they stood a chance. Each was probably overconfident in the abilities of the other.

The biggest of the gang members sat up high on a bar running across the bench like he was on some sort of throne. Big Red, they called him. A nasty piece of work which usually gave the orders but didn't get his own hands dirty. When he did, though, he was a savage. Making sure to prove his point; that there was a reason people did what he commanded.

"What you gonna do, Lomax? Take us all on?" Red growled.

"Well, I came here for a workout," Scott replied with an outtake of breath, his deep gravelly voice was unshakable with a calm confidence.

"You really gonna make something of this just for Talcum X over here?" Red sniggered as he spoke with echoes of laughter from the rest of the gang that dried up and went serious again in less than a second.

All eyes were back on Lomax.

Scott pulled the towel from around his neck and threw it aside. In less than a second, the gang members piled onto Scott, and he erupted like a volcano. The man mountain exploded like some kind of a wild beast, taking all seven inmates on at once. Making a point of plowing through them all to go after Red. He took the blows as he forced himself forward.

He knocked Red off his perch and grabbed his head, clamping his huge hands on either side of Red's scalp. The bench bar and weights toppled over with the clanging of metal hitting each other before landing on the floor.

Lomax drove a hard knee to the ribs, a headbutt following less than a second later. Red took a deep breath and slapped his arms up on top of Scott's in defense, but Scott was already about to take him out.

Still being whacked from every angle, Scott ignored the blows and pushed his thumbs inward across Red's face. The noise of the shouting seemed distant as Scott slid his thumbs across Red's slippery skin. Sliding through the sweat until he found the soft area under the eyes. He put the pressure on and curled his thumbs so they were positioned on either side of Red's nose. His thumb nails pierced the skin near the tear ducts, and Red screamed as Scott pushed in, splitting the eyelid skin and curling his thumbs around the back of Red's slippery wet eyeballs. The scream was deafening, and Red jerked and thrashed.

Then Red's eyeballs popped out and Scott left them dangling. Red dropped to the floor, passed out from the pain and shock.

The others hadn't stopped jabbing fists into Scott and whacking him from every angle. Scott turned with a fierce look in his eyes and snarled as he picked the one who was having it next. Each of the gang members took crippling blows from Scott as he tore through them all. He ran into the next guy and gripped his shirt, not stopping as they collided but speeding up. Scott kept plowing forward at high speed, sending the guys back, crashing into the full-length mirror on the wall. The big guy dropped for a moment, and Scott decided to carry on with the rest of them. Pounding into them and throwing them around. As huge as some of them were, Scott's fists and feet smashed into them. Even the bigger men were thrown like rag dolls over gym equipment and into the walls. They'd hit the floor and scramble up to have another attempt at taking him on, but Scott just kept plowing into them, taking any hits that were dished and causing as much damage to each of them as he could, kneeing, punching and smashing each inmate into bloody submission.

It hadn't taken him long to reduce the gang to the last remaining three members, all of which were now looking the worse for wear. Scott himself had taken a pounding but, despite his cuts and bruises, stood ready for the next round, breathing heavily and showing his teeth in anger.

Then the guards swarmed into the room. One of the overzealous guards tried to restrain Scott. That was his first mistake. Scott threw him off like an angry gorilla tossing away a rotten piece of meat. The guard jumped back up and pulled out a Taser. That was his second mistake. Scott snarled as he gave him a look of warning, which had the opposite of the desired effect. It was fear that made the guard shoot the Taser. The barbed probes pierced Scott's skin and dug into the flesh of his chest. Scott's nose crinkled as his anger surfaced. A look of sheer rage filled his eyes. The second wave of fear had the guard making his last mistake. He pulled the trigger and sent a shock down the curled wires and into Scott's body.

Scott roared as he ripped the barbed probes from his chest and wound the wires around his arm. His vision tunneled as he marched toward the guard with only one intention. A newbie stepped in between them. It was time for him to make *his* first mistake. The newbie sprayed mace into Scott's face, which only served to anger him more. Scott's face contorted like an animal. Grabbing the newbie's throat and then gripping the guard still holding the Taser for dear life, he smashed their heads together several times, like a cymbal player in a band. Smashing the two guards into the wall, he was about to dish out the next serving when more guards in full riot gear stormed in and jumped on him.

After three sedative injections and nearly two hours of fighting off guards in full body armor and protective helmets and face guards, they finally managed to wear him down enough to drag him to solitary confinement. The once-beige anti-slip cushion flooring of the prison gym was awash with red. There was so much blood it was impossible to know whose was whose.

Scott didn't even realize in the midst of the fighting that he'd actually killed two of the gang members. Not that he'd have shown any remorse for them. The young lad in the gym who was being bullied was having his life traded away for tobacco. A few packs of cigarettes and pouches of rolling tobacco and that kid was going to be someone's nightly abused prison slave and sex toy. He'd watched as the kid, Nathan, was pushed around the gym and physically degraded until, eventually, Scott snapped.

Scott didn't even know who the kid was. He didn't have to. He had a son only a few years younger, and the thought of his son going through anything like this was enough of a catalyst to make him lash out. The remaining gang members who survived were all in the infirmary. Eight guards had ended up hospitalized, and eleven others were sent home.

Scott was not popular in prison today—or on any other day. He was not liked by the other inmates and was not liked by the guards. But he wasn't there to make friends.

He sat in solitary confinement in the dark, disheveled, battered, and bruised.

A few days in the box, and then he could get out, back into gen-pop.

Once there, he could finish the job.

Chapter 2

Manicured lush green lawns encompassed Neil Frampton's multi-million dollar house. The huge white imposing property was like something from a *Dream Home* glossy magazine. As the CEO of one of America's largest pharmaceutical companies, he was no stranger to the finer things in life.

Not a single hair on his head was out of place as he leaned back into his designer leather office chair. A crystal glass sat two-thirds full of his wife's homemade fruit smoothie. The soft pinky-white skin of his hands looked like he'd never even known what a callous was. He sat relaxed, talking with his board members from the comfort of his home office. Luxury was a standard setting in Neil's life. He leaned back a little farther in his chair as his board members made all the right noises to top off the start off what was so far a perfect day.

Without warning, his video conference was rudely interrupted. The screen in front of him went blank, and the large wall-mounted TV lit up with a pixelated face.

"Pay attention, Neil," the robotic voice commanded.

"What the hell? Who the hell are you?" Neil growled at the TV.

"I'm your worst nightmare, Neil. I'm going to give you a list of instructions. And you will do exactly what I tell you."

"The hell I will!"

"Look out of the window. I'll show you why you're going to do everything I tell you."

Neil looked outside to see his two children playing with their nanny. His heart beat increased for a moment as anger preceded thoughts of dread. He watched closely as panic filled his mind. His two beautiful children played in the mid-afternoon sun, running around their nanny. Playful screams and laughter could be heard as they chased each other. Neil watched carefully in fear of what could possibly be coming. The pause seemed to last an eternity.

Then, time stopped.

The nanny stood bolt upright. The children, unaware anything was wrong, still ran in circles around her. She shook violently. Appearing to have some kind of a seizure before collapsing to the ground.

The children carried on running in rings for a moment, thinking she was still playing. Neil stared intensely out of the window. A mixture of relief that his children were okay and grief for the nanny, as well as the shock of watching her die in front of him, had unimaginable thoughts swirling around in his mind. His thoughts were abruptly interrupted.

"I have the ability to get to anyone, anywhere, at any time. Completely remotely. And *this* is why you are going to do what I want. Because if you don't, next time, it will be one of your loved ones."

Rational thinking was almost impossible for Neil at that moment. Somehow he managed to keep it together. It was not a time for getting hot-headed or making threats or demands. He'd been caught off guard. Right now, he needed to get a grip on the situation and come to terms with how to deal with this. He made a split-second decision to agree. Buy himself some time. He was in a grave situation that had shaken him to the core. Seeing the nanny die in front of his eyes by a remote killer was terrifying, if not least for the fact that it showed him exactly how vulnerable he and his family were.

"Okay, okay, I'll do whatever you want. Anything." Neil swallowed as he spoke quietly. Still in partial shock.

"You are to turn everything you have into crypto currency. Liquidate every asset and use every penny you've got. When it's all turned into crypto currency, I'll be in touch and tell you what I want you to do next. I'll call again in seventy-two hours." The voice stopped, and the screen went black.

Neil flopped into his office chair. Unable to speak, unable to think. Just a blank expression on his face. The playing outside stopped. His children stood on either side of their nanny. They finally realized she wasn't playing and that something was drastically wrong.

Neil jumped back into the present moment, then ran through the house to get outside to his children. He called his wife as he ran.

"Lucy!" Neil yelled. "Lucy, quickly!" He burst through the rear door to get to the garden. She caught up to him as Neil skidded to his knees at the side of the nanny. "Go inside," he said to his children before turning back to his wife. "Call an ambulance!"

"What happened?" Lucy asked, the panic evident in her voice as she scrambled to dial 911. Lucy had seen enough of death in recent years, and her emotions were in turmoil.

Lucy's grandparents were immigrants to the US from Ireland. They came over with nothing and worked themselves to the bone to provide for their children. Two generations on and Lucy was the well-mannered daughter of a proud, hard-working father. Again they never had much, but she'd been brought up with integrity and love. When she met Neil, her life changed. Every ounce of happiness comes with a price though it seems. Three years into marriage, she and Neil had been trying for a baby with no luck. Copious amounts of fertility treatment had her to the point of almost giving up when one day, a miracle happened. She conceived her son. Thinking she could never be any happier, only months after her son was born, she discovered she was pregnant for a second time with the daughter she'd always wanted.

Living a life of perfection didn't last long, though. A year later, her mother passed away from cancer, sending her into a downward spiral of depression and anxiety. This was followed by a cancer scare of her own. The handpicked nanny was brought in to help, and when Lucy was finally given the all-clear, life to her seemed more beautiful in every way.

She enveloped herself in life. A new found joy for every moment that passed. Her appreciation for existence was brimming from her. She stood with tears in her eyes as she called the ambulance for the nanny, who'd not only helped her through her dark times but also become her closest friend.

The nanny was still giving the odd flinching reaction. Her skin had turned the palest shade of white. She lay still on the brilliant green grass, her dark hair wet and her body looking like an empty vessel that had been drained of every ounce of life. An eerie vacantness about her shook Neil to the core. She did not look like someone who had just died moments ago but more like someone who had ben dead years, been frozen, and now just defrosted in front of him. The scene that was unfolding made concern for his family grow infinitely.

Neil looked up at his beautiful wife, barely holding it together as she spoke on the phone. She'd been through enough. He was going to find whoever was responsible and make them pay. His wife did not deserve this.

She had always said she was the lucky one to meet her tall, dark, and handsome prince charming. A powerful and wonderful man with money who doted upon her and blessed her with two beautiful children and a magnificent life. Neil felt it was the other way around, though. His gorgeous wife was not a typical lady of leisure. She demanded nothing and was grateful for all they had. She worked as a volunteer at the animal shelter just because of her love for animals and her longing to help those less fortunate—whether it was animals or people. That was why she had picked the nanny out, not because of her qualifications but unlike the other candidates, this job would be life-changing for her.

It was the love inside that made Lucy more beautiful to Neil. She was made of something different. Something more valuable than any amount of money. He loved her wholeheartedly, and seeing her in tears yet again was physically hurting him. He looked up at her, listening intently to the voice of the emergency operator on the other end of the phone. He took her hand and held her shaking palm. His emotions overwhelmed him and finally escaped in the form of small tears that trickled from the corners of his eyes.

"It's going to be okay," he whispered to her, but she hadn't heard him. Like always, she was so concerned about putting other people first. She was too engrossed with helping to think about herself. It was at that point Neil decided he was going to protect his family and get justice for what had been done. He would keep the details of this situation away from her. She didn't need any more stress.

Neil was going to do everything in his power to resolve this atrocity once and for all.

Chapter 3

Scott wasn't sure exactly how long he'd been in solitary. It didn't matter much. The longer he was in this dark, dingy hole, the more his wounds healed. His senses were starting to sharpen again, too. Despite the sleep deprivation that the guards were trying to enforce on him, randomly blasting the lights and making announcements over the tannoy, Scott was recomposing his mental stance. The comparison of how his head felt when he entered solitary to now was almost immeasurable. Instead of being awoken by the sound of a meal being slammed through the hatch of the cell door and slid across the floor, he was now sharp, primed, and poised to react to everything going on around him. The mere sound of the key clicking the door lock at the end of the corridor had his ears pricking up and on full alert.

He'd learned to identify each individual guard whenever they approached. Not just the footsteps but other subtle tells that Scott's enhanced senses honed while he was locked in his dark hole. The throat clears, the jangles of keys and patterns of people's habits. Some preferred to walk to the door and wait before reaching for their keys. Others preferred to have their keys waiting in their hands, held tight before unlocking the hatch. One in particular, though, would run his forefinger through the loop, swing the keys and catch them in his palm before using the rest of his fingers to maneuver them to the back of the ring again and repeat the process for the entire walk to the cell.

That same guard had two other distinguishing features. The scent of cheap cologne so heavily applied it could almost be perceived as some form of overcompensation. The first, however, was explained by the next. He frequently sniffed. He sniffed as he talked, he sniffed as he walked, and he sniffed with each breath on some occasions.

Scott had equated that he was having a bit too much fun in the snow at parties that weren't for skiing. Over-indulgence in the white stuff had dampened his sense of smell, hence the mid-life crisis quantities of cologne.

It was this guy he hated more than the others. Logic equated to this guy cashing in on the prison gang's nefarious activities. Not only was he more than likely actively participating, but he was on the wrong side of the bars, in Scott's opinion. The double standards and irony of this guy personally punishing the people who were incarcerated for doing exactly what he was actively engaging in was despicable.

For the rest of the world, the clock was ticking through the average day. For Scott, he was psychologically prepared for the day the door swung open. Time didn't matter. Some form of exercise would have been advantageous, but it wasn't his top priority. He could still stretch his limbs when he got out. It wouldn't take him long to loosen up. Then he'd finish what he started and break down the rest of the gang. If a handful of the corrupt prison guards got caught in the crossfire, then that was just a bonus.

His bruises were fading, and the cuts were healing. His body was returning to full strength. Since being thrown in the hole, the growth on Scott's face was too long to be stubble but too short to be considered a beard. Like the hair on his head, it was mostly dark brown, but the odd light-colored, pre-gray hair attempted to sneak through. Today, they were camouflaged by dried blood.

Footsteps approaching his cell brought him back to the present moment. He sat up and watched the door. No movement. No sounds. Then a tell-tale sniff preceded a voice from the other side.

"Hey, Lomax? I know you can hear me." The guard paused for a brief moment. "Well, just to let you know, that kid, Nathan, you were fighting to defend in the gym, word is they're going to pass him around the showers tonight before they shank the little bastard. So all that scrapping you did, to wind up getting your ass locked up in here, it was for nothin'!" The guard growled.

"Don't let anything happen to that kid. You hear me?" Scott shouted, but there was no reply. "You hear me? Anything happens to that kid, and I'm going to destroy every last one of you!" Scott's rage boiled over as he paced the tiny dark cell, powerless to do anything to protect the kid. The familiar smell of cheap cologne wafted into his cell as Scott approached boiling point near the cold steel cell door.

The offensive scent detonated Scott's rage. The pressure of his boiling temper was ready to explode with nowhere to go.

Arms by his sides, veins pumped in his massive forearms, his fists clenched, he looked up, erupting with a roar of frustration. An aggressive glint in his eye lit up like it was full of a powerful force ready to explode when unleashed on the chosen prey.

* * *

With the deadline looming, Neil had gone to the extent he believed to be more than necessary to secure his family and fortune from the clutches of some psychotic freak with remote sniper skills. He'd carefully approached high-powered and well-placed friends with the best personal security on the market. High-profile entrepreneurs and businessmen were frequently the targets of ransom. With every phone call Neil made, his confidence swelled.

He assembled a team ready and waiting in the wings for a signal, and they would execute their craft with surgical precision. Hired specialists of everybody from ex-Special Forces to the world's most articulate hostage negotiator who was on standby as Neil prepared to negotiate the future of his family and legacy with an unknown enemy.

Neil's sleek designer desk phone rang, and the negotiator glanced his way. Neil's eyes were naturally filled with panic, but the negotiator reassured him. He came highly recommended, and the silver-tongued negotiator had managed to ease Neil's fears with his articulate mannerisms and amazing ability to instantly have the right answers to every question. It almost gave Neil a sense of empowerment once again that he'd managed to take control of the situation somewhat. That was what ultimately swung the decision to not tell his wife of the situation until after it had been dealt with. He would pay the high price of the best negotiator available, deal with the blackmailer and send in his highly-trained team to find him and deliver vengeance for the threats upon his family.

He might have to play it meek and mild for the moment, but soon enough, the tables would be turned. Right now, though, he just had to rely on the phenomenal skills of the professional negotiator who sat in front of him. Calm, collected, and prepared, the negotiator answered the phone, looking at Neil with an expression of reassurance.

"Put Neil on," the disguised voice demanded.

"Of course. I'll get him on the line as you desire, but as I do, I'd like to extend the invitation to ..." The negotiator stopped talking and went rigid. Shaking violently, like some kind of exorcism was taking place. His eyes filled with blood. He dropped the handset of the phone in fits of violent spasms. The negotiator fell to the floor and stopped moving like somebody had hit an off switch. He lay still. Pale white. No breath, no movement. Dead.

Neil picked up the handset of the phone. His mouth went dry. All the feelings of control he'd convinced himself he had now slipped away. He became sticky as he perspired. A dribble of sweat trickled down the small of his back, forming a wet patch and making his shirt stick to his skin. His pulse quickened. He went light-headed as he stood up too fast. He gulped and slowly moved the handset to his ear like it could explode if it came into contact with the side of his head. Holding it less than a millimeter away from his face, he tried his best to control his shaking hand before he finally spoke.

"Hello?" Neil's shaky voice croaked.

"Your negotiator is not needed. You didn't do what I asked you to do, did you?" The robot-like voice came clearly down the line.

Neil said nothing. Too many possible answers flooded his mind, and as quickly as he thought of them, he dismissed them for fear of saying the wrong thing. For the first time in his life, Neil Frampton felt so far out of his depth that he was literally stuck for words.

"Did you think I was playing, Neil? I told you what I wanted you to do, and you haven't done it. I know everything you get up to. You didn't convert anything to cryptocurrency. So, for your disobedience, you will have to pay the price. You have two beautiful children, Neil. Pick one."

Chapter 4

Neil's mind raced. How could he pick one of his children? His stomach knotted and churned as so many questions swirled in his mind. If he were to pick one, would that be the one that was let live or the one this man killed? Either way, he couldn't do it. He could never decide between his two children. He would never be able to live with himself, no matter what the result. He went weak in the knees. He shook from head to toe. A dry lump in his throat formed as the seals of his tear ducts broke and leaked out his fears.

His bottom lip quivered as he spoke. "I can't." Neil sobbed. "I can't do it. Please, I'll do anything. Please."

"Every penny, Neil! Every penny! Turn it into cryptocurrency!" the voice commanded. "You better do it this time! Everything, I want it all. Transfer it all to me, and I'll let your children live." The voice calmed a little before continuing. "Don't waste time, Neil. I want you to get this sorted. The clock's ticking. I'll call back in forty-eight hours, but first, you need to learn a lesson. You need to know how serious I am. You better get to the kitchen and say goodbye to your wife." The line went dead.

"Lucy!" Neil yelled, dropping the phone and running through the house. "Lucy!" He shouted once more as he scrambled to get into the kitchen.

When he burst through the door, she turned to face him.

"What's wrong?" she asked, a look of concern filling her face as he dived at her, wrapping his arms around her.

"Oh, Lucy, thank the lord you're okay."

"Of course, I'm okay," she replied

"I love you." He held her tight as the fear subsided and relief took over. "I love you so much, Lucy."

"I love you, too," she said as she held him tight.

He couldn't let her go. He was so terrified that he'd nearly lost her that he didn't want to release his grip. His eyes were filled with tears as he continued to hug her. At first, he thought the trembles were from Lucy starting to cry. Then they quickened, became more violent.

"No!" He moved back, still gripping her with a hand on each of her shoulders. "No! Please, no!"

Her eyes rolled into the back of her head, filling with blood. The color drained from her as the spasms began, and she thrashed out of control before dropping to the floor, lifeless.

"*No!*"

Chapter 5

Raymond Napier inspected the increased balance of his cryptocurrency funds, the corners of his mouth curling upward in a display of satisfaction. The fact that he'd financially crippled a CEO of a pharmaceutical company in the process was just a bonus to him. He was already a wealthy man, but the increased funds would ease the way for him to move his plan to the next level.

"It's nearly time." He watched his wife Lina gracefully walk into the room and descend onto the luxurious chaise longue in the enormous castle they had recently come to call home. Built by a wine merchant at the foot of his vineyard, the thirteenth-century Tuscan castle-style building was Napier's new home. Being a wine connoisseur was what first peaked his interest. He'd previously remained on his super luxury yacht, *Naughty-Cull Dream*, until an excursion for a few days in California, where they discovered the beautiful castle they now called home. Napier and his wife were visiting Napa valley for a wine-tasting experience and fell in love with the place. Napier being the man he was, wouldn't take no for an answer when he made an offer to buy the place. And just like anything else in his life, if he wanted it, he took it. His ownership was covered by so many nefarious means that had enabled him to remain off the grid.

Napier and his wife remained impossible to trace.

He'd met his wife years ago while studying medicine in Germany. She fell for him instantly when she saw a passion in him like in no other man she'd seen before. He had a fire, a drive. He had a purpose and a direction in his life. She could tell when she talked to him that he was dedicated to fulfilling his purpose. She could also clearly see the determination to get there. It was that passion alone that drew her to him. She had watched him set goals and ruthlessly reach them, each goal he set taking him higher in his rise to his final target. Now she watched as he neared his goals. For so many years, she'd watched him so intently through infatuated eyes that she could see no bad in him, no matter what he did to reach his goal. As his journey progressed, his power grew, and that acted as more of an aphrodisiac, making her want him even more. The beautiful German girl with the palest of skin and the longest of silky black hair watched her husband with admiration through her liquid-like, dark brown eyes, lit up with love and desire.

"The system they use is flawed," Napier said.

Lina had heard it so many times before, but she loved to hear the passion in his voice. He was on fire. He was never so alive as when he had made progress in his plans.

"Medication and profits, that's all they care about, not cures. The pills they force onto these poor unwitting people don't even fix them. They simply alleviate the symptoms, not solve the problem. And then comes the side effects from yet another pill they're taking. And what do healthcare professionals do? Do they try to find the root of the problem? Do they spend time with their patients trying to determine the cause? No. They prescribe more pills! And why? Money! More and more money. The healthcare system is driven by pure greed. Doctors are getting commissions for pushing drugs onto the sick. The very man you trust with your health is the very man who profits from your illness. Of course, he's not going to cure you. People who are cured don't make the system money." Napier was on a roll, giving his spiel to his adoring wife like he was giving a speech at an award ceremony. "So they keep you coming back for more and more pills. And if anyone dares to challenge the system, if anyone attempts to actually find the means of preventing or eradicating a virus, they are silenced by the powers that be. Well, soon, that will all come to an end, as the powers that be will answer to me!"

Napier picked up a glass of his homegrown wine, pausing only for a moment to hold it below his nose and appreciate the scent of the fine claret. He closed his eyes as he inhaled, holding it before finally releasing his breath. He looked at his wife and raised his glass before taking a sip. "I will change the world," he said, and she really believed he would, too. She had as much conviction and faith in her husband as he did in himself. He clinked glasses with his wife as they smiled at each other.

"Ya, zat you vill," she agreed.

Napier's toast was interrupted by a knock at the door. The person on the other side didn't wait for an answer before entering.

"Ah, Douglas," Napier said with a tone of satisfaction.

Douglas Wilde entered the room, pleased to be delivering good news to his boss. Napier had initially hired him as a bodyguard and to be the muscle of the operation but soon found Douglas had many other talents, too. The herculean man was a powerhouse with a short fuse. A scar ran from the top of his forehead down the side of his face, in the shape of an upside-down letter Y. It curled around the bottom of his chin, and the top led to more scars where flaps of skin had knitted back together and become hidden by the short hairs on his head. An explosion where he was the only survivor in a Middle Eastern conflict zone was behind his brutal mannerisms and many battle scars. As the pilot of a helicopter shot down in

Iraq, he was lucky to have survived the explosion, never mind the attack that followed. He single-handedly held off attacks from multiple directions before finally being captured and tortured.

When the time was right, he made his escape, but not before killing every single one of his captors in the middle of the night. The one that had watched as Douglas was tortured, he saved until last. He bit the man's throat out and spat it on the floor in a rage. Douglas Wilde was a ferocious killer. Wilde by name and wild by nature. His vicious temper was now contained, only to be unleashed when Napier saw it necessary. His military background, followed by incarceration, made Wilde a unique beast. Napier had shown him rewards for his work that he'd never experienced before. He soon adopted

Napier's outlook and completed whatever was required of him with an emotionless sense of duty.

"The entire list is now complete, sir," Douglas grunted.

"Every name?" Napier asked, already confident in Douglas's reply before he'd said it.

"Every single one, all taken care of." Douglas handed a dark blue flash drive to Napier.

"Excellent!" Napier cheered. "Well done. Let's celebrate." Napier made his way over to the wine bottle. He poured another glass. Douglas wrapped his giant, cobweb-scarred hand around the wine glass and joined Napier in a toast.

Chapter 6

The Director of National Intelligence, Charles Driskel, gripped the dark blue flash drive tightly as he paced through the grounds of the White House. His sharp suit reflected the image he portrayed; money and power. His white hair was the only giveaway of his age. His height allowed for easy long, and rapid strides as he made his way through the White House corridors. People parted like the waves for Moses as Charles powered his way along with a look of purpose to what would probably be the most important meeting of his life.

The president and his staff, along with a select few others, were all expecting his arrival and waited impatiently in the Situation Room. He burst through the door and was instantly bombarded with questions.

"What the hell's going on that's so urgent you've got us all gathered here waiting for you like a bunch of—" The secretary of state was interrupted by the DNI.

"Sit down!" he bellowed. "I'll show you!" He lifted the flash drive to show it to everyone in the room. "I got this earlier this morning. Watch carefully." The DNI inserted the drive into a port that allowed the contents to be brought up on the large screen in front of them. "We have verified this threat is credible and real." With a couple of clicks the video played.

"My name is Raymond Napier. My father named me after a man called Royal Raymond Rife. A genius born in 1888 whom most people probably won't have heard of. That's the exact reason for this video and the exact reason I'm about to do what I'm going to do."

Looks of confusion filled the room, but everyone carried on watching the screen regardless. Nobody was sure what was about to follow, but they were all certain that whatever it was, it wasn't going to be good.

"Royal Raymond Rife was the forgotten genius of the 1920s and thirties. He discovered the cure for all viruses. Through his own invention, the Rife microscope, he was able to view viruses in real-time. He figured out that by taking a blood sample and placing it under his microscope, he could run through a series of light frequencies, and different organisms, viruses, and bacteria in the blood would illuminate, identifying the virus. By identifying the type of virus, he simply found the corresponding sound frequency and bombarded the virus with it. The virus would then shatter like a crystal glass does on high C."

There was a growing impatience in the Situation Room. Why were they watching a video of some nutty professor giving them a history lesson? They looked toward the DNI as if he might give an answer, but he simply pointed a finger at the screen to keep watching, as if he could read their thoughts.

"Royal Raymond Rife was a real medical genius. Healing so many people. Banquets were given to celebrate the end of all diseases. But that was not good news for the men of power. If disease was ended, what would the doctors do? If there was no disease, the drug manufacturers would be out of business. The pharmaceutical companies would be destroyed. So Rife was discredited. False claims of fraud, he was made out to be a madman. Banished from the medical community. The U.S. government destroyed him. Took all of his designs for his inventions and destroyed everything he had stood for." Napier paused for a moment to compose himself. "My father carried on his work, only to fall victim to the same fate two decades later. The U.S. government stole his patents, took his devices, and, yet again, discredited the work of a good man trying to make the world a better place. He was thrown into prison for crimes that were never defined and eventually hung himself, seeing himself as a failure. He'd failed to bring to the world the means of healing diseases that he had promised to produce."

"What's ..." A voice called out from the back of the room, but the DNI made a shush sound and placed his finger over his mouth, then pointing back at the screen.

"I realized that if I was going to bring this technology into the world, I had to go a very different route, or I too would fall victim to the same fate as my father and that of Rife. I came to see the American government only understands one language, the language of threats and power. So I took the devices invented by Rife and the ones reproduced by my father and weaponized them. I tested their power and perfected them with great results. And to prove how powerful they are and to ensure you meet my demands, I will give you a demonstration. At exactly 1600 hours today, I will kill the secretary of defense!"

All eyes in the room turned to the SecDef, Gregory Kessler. He stood proud in his medal-covered uniform but could not disguise his immediate concern and, as quietly as he could, swallowed. In an attempt to cover his fear, he stood tall and pushed his shoulders back.

"It's probably just an empty threat. The guy's a nut job. How's he going to even get near me?" Kessler asked, looking at Charles Driskel as if he had the answers. The voice coming from the screen continued.

"You will witness firsthand that no matter what you do, all of your soldiers, all of your agents, no matter where you take him, nothing will protect him. You will see that I have the ability to execute anyone, anywhere, at any time!" There was a pause before Napier continued. "Attached to this flash drive is a list of ten thousand names. Ten thousand American citizens, whom I will execute forty-eight hours after the secretary of defense's death. The biggest attack in American history is imminent, and the only way to stop it is if you meet the demands I will lay out for you!"

Charles Driskel paused the video. He turned the lights back up in the Situation Room. Everyone had questions, but the silence lasted. Eventually, the president spoke.

"Get Gregory to Camp David!" he ordered. "What does he want?" The president turned his attention to the DNI.

"A whole bunch of stuff. Most of it was impossible. He wants all pharmaceutical companies to be made into non-profit organizations that develop cures instead of medications. The current boards and CEOs of said companies are to be tried for crimes against humanity. He wants their full confession televised, as they acknowledge their part in profiting from illness and withholding means of cures, for profits and gains. And that's the easy stuff. The guy's a fruit."

"Find him. Find him now!" the president commanded. "By any means necessary. I want this man found yesterday."

"There may be ways, but ..." Charles Driskel paused for a moment. "They're not applicable if I have to continue under current legal restrictions."

"We're facing the largest terrorist attack on American soil, by none other than a homegrown psychopath, with the potential means of killing thousands of innocent civilians. I don't care what you have to do—get this man!"

Within the hour, Gregory Kessler had boarded Marine 1 and been flown immediately to Camp David. Masses of militarized agents and secret service members worked in every possible way they could to plan for the attack. He paced as he watched the clock ticking.

"Ah, I'm not going to sit around here waiting to die!" Gregory said, marching toward the door leading to the lush gardens.

"Sir, no." Gary Johnson, team leader of his personal security detail, called out in an attempt to get Gregory to stay inside. The display on the kitchen clock showed 15:57.

"It's fine. Look around you, Gary. Nobody's going to even get close to me." Gregory looked at his watch: 15:58. "I'm going for a cigarette." He extracted one from his pack.

"Sir, could you just wait until after 16:00? Just so we can relax a little knowing the threat has passed?" Gary's look of concern displayed on his forehead as he raised his eyebrows and waited for Gregory to respond.

"If I'm going to die, I want to enjoy one last smoke before I go!" Gregory stated and continued to walk toward the back door.

Chapter 7

"Please, sir?" Gary stood in his way, holding a hand up just short of Gregory's chest.

The secretary of defense placed his unlit cigarette in his mouth and looked around him. Weighing the options of whether or not it would matter if he lit it up inside. He decided he didn't care. If he died, it wouldn't matter, and if he lived, he was pretty sure he was going to be forgiven under the circumstances. He pulled his lighter from his pocket and looked at his watch: 15:59.

"Why of all the people in the White House did he pick me?" Gregory asked.

"What, sir?"

"Oh, nothing, I was just thinking out loud," he said, lighting his cigarette and taking a long draw in before exhaling a cloud of smoke in the palatial abode.

"You think he's making a statement?" Gary asked. "The man in charge of defense? That kind of thing?"

Gregory looked at his watch: 16:01.

"See, what did I tell you? Just a hoax by another nut job." Gregory took another long draw on his cigarette and blew twin plumes of smoke from his nose. A second later, he coughed.

Gary was still distracted by Gregory's question to notice his coughing lasted longer than it should have. Nobody reacted at first. They just thought he'd choked on a bit too much smoke. Then the convulsions started.

He shook violently, and his eyeballs rolled backward. He fell to the floor, and his body thrashed like he was having a seizure.

"Sir!" Gary dived in to see if he could do anything to assist Gregory but was helpless to stop the attack. It was at this point the rest of the Secret Service team members realized what was going on.

* * *

Three prison guards in full body armor and helmets nervously poised to open Scott's cell door. They were braced like they were about to let a giant rabid dog out of its cage. Twenty-five more guards on standby stood waiting on the other side of a locked door, ready to dive in if Scott attacked.

The first guard slid the bolt back with a clang that echoed through the corridor. He pulled and swung the heavy door open, stepping back against the wall. Scott calmly walked out and turned right to face the open door at the other end of the corridor. All he had to do was walk out of the door at the far end, and the nervous guards could close the door behind him and return to safety, back in their guard room.

Scott walked the freshly mopped corridor, the slight scent of bleach still lingering and the chalky white water marks still vaguely visible on the floor. His steps echoed as he approached the lit-up doorway. Back into gen-pop. Back into the place he wanted to be. Back to the place where he could do everything he'd been thinking about for every second he had spent in solitary confinement.

Scott walked into the main dining area, and all eyes were fixed on him. The smell of sweaty bodies and mass-catered food merged to drown out the scent of the cleaning chemicals that were now fading. The clinking and chewing seemed to stop, and the whole dining hall stared as he walked up the middle.

"Hey, Lomax," a huge guy said, looking right at Scott. "That kid?" He made a slicing action with his index finger across the front of his own neck, making a sound in the back of his throat.

Lomax felt a rage blasting through him. He tried his best to control it, but the fury started to fill him up, every limb now engorged and primed.

His blood was boiling as it surged through his veins, every muscle taught feeling like he was on fire. A burst of aggression was being held back and contained with every ounce of strength he had.

"He's getting out of the infirmary later, he's dead tonight!" The big guy growled.

That was enough to light his fuse. Scott exploded, diving forward swiftly, delivering a lightning speed throat punch with the speed and accuracy of a striking viper, knocking the big guy backward off his chair. The big guy stood, coughing and grabbing his throat.

Scott didn't waste any time. He launched himself forward and, putting all his weight on his back leg, drew his front leg up and kicked down just above the big guy's ankle, transferring weight forward as he did it. The sickening crunch of bone breaking was like a thick piece of timber being hit by a sledgehammer. The big guy dropped instantly. The pain didn't even give him a chance to scream. He passed out when he hit the floor. Scott was now pumped with adrenaline and in attack mode. He'd decked the big guy, and masses of gang members were poised and waiting for action. Scott ran forward and hoofed an almighty kick in the guts to the big guy to make sure he felt it when he finally came around. That was the catalyst of what was about to happen.

The dining hall erupted into a riot as inmates rushed toward Scott. The crowds gathered in a growing circle around him, each of them swinging a punch or kicking out. Scott felt the blows but was too busy reaching out to get a grip on the main man. Scott managed to grab the main guy by his lapel, and despite the constant blows that were pounding away at Scott's body from every direction, he laid into the main man. Pummelling his face with punch after punch.

* * *

Agent Carver drove toward the prison the fastest he'd ever gone without having his lights and siren on. He'd already gotten into trouble twice that day. The first time was sending a call up the line to define "Any means necessary," and as the question went up, the yells came back down twice as loud, shouting "Any means necessary!"

The second was when he was still in the FBI field office after finding this out. He should have been out doing whatever he could to put into action whatever prompted this question.

The AC battled to cool the car's interior as Carver raced along the freeway. A small wet patch at the back of his shirt irritated him as it stuck to his skin when he leaned forward, fidgeting in his chair. He felt uncomfortable with the direction the day was taking. Steadying his breathing, he was doing his best to remain calm and answer the questions from his superior, who was on speakerphone.

"So, who exactly *is* this, Scott Lomax?" the crackling voice asked over the car's loudspeaker.

"He used to be an operative and a damn good one, too," Carver replied.

"Not only is he highly trained, but he's a freak of nature. A dangerous one at that. He has inhuman endurance and a mental skillset to match. He was a secret governmental weapon and one of the best ones they had. Up until his wife died, that is. Then he went off the rails. Now, he's an unhinged, uncontrollable, violent, and rage-filled monster."

"Sounds like a charmer. And why exactly are we getting him involved?"

"Because of the recommendations to use any means necessary. He might be a monster, but he's a useful monster. When an unstoppable force meets an immovable object, you get Scott Lomax! He doesn't know the meaning of the word fail and will go above and beyond the measure of any human alive to find this guy. Better than anyone else on the planet. Especially when I tell him what's at stake."

"Well, you've been hand-picked and specially selected to be the SAC on this, Carver, so I hope you know what you're doing. He's your responsibility, I really hope you can control this guy."

"*Nobody* can control this guy!" Carver replied as he changed to the inside lane, ready to race up the exit ramp.

"Well, you better do something!"

"Best I can do is put somebody with him to try and regulate the collateral damage."

"Do you have somebody in mind?"

"I have someone in place. Although, like I said, it will only be damage limitation at best. Lomax is an atomic bomb, and I'll be sending a fire truck to deal with the fall out."

The tires of his car screeched as he left the freeway and rallied around the exit ramp's hot tarmac onto the main road. Weaving between the traffic, he thrashed the car at high speed. The engine screamed, lights flashing, and the siren wailing.

"But he'll definitely get the job done?"

"I'd bet my lefticle on it!" Carver said.

The call ended, and Carver skidded to a halt in the parking lot. The engine made a ticking sound as it cooled after being turned off. The prison warden had been notified ahead of Carver's imminent arrival, so it was not a surprise when he was rushed through security and straight up to the governor's office.

The varnished wooden panel on the walls in the governor's office was a huge difference from the rest of the concrete and plain prison rooms and buildings. It looked more like a Texas roadhouse than an office. Taxidermies of various-sized animals dotted the walls, all probably hunting trophies. The smell of extinguished cigars lingered over the waft of black coffee.

"I need to speak to Scott Lomax immediately," Carver told him.

"I'm not sure that's going to be possible right now," the governor said with a half-smile. His leather button-back chair creaked as he leaned back in it slightly.

Carver wasn't sure why he was holding back. He'd been told this was a matter of extreme urgency and sensed the governor was creating an unnecessary block of Carver's progress. Carver unfolded a document and handed it to the governor.

"I'm afraid I'm going to have to insist," Carver said as he leaned forward and took the paper in his hands, easing the strain on his office chair as it creaked once more. The governor read the paper and dropped it on the desk in front of him.

"Okay, but don't say I didn't warn you." The governor held up his hands as he stood. He walked around this desk and led Carver through the prison to a door where guards in riot gear seemed to be waiting for the right moment to enter.

"Open it!" the governor commanded. A guard flung the door open to show a mass brawl in the dining hall. Injured and unconscious inmates lay spread out everywhere, and the fight seemed to center around one person.

Carver walked in amongst the chaos.

"Lomax," he said sternly, but nothing changed. "Lomax!" he shouted even louder. Still, the fighting continued.

Carver pulled out his pistol. He looked over to an area to his left that would absorb the bullet without causing any damage. Carver shot a round-off that ricocheted off the floor before being absorbed by the plaster of the wall, not making it past the brick behind the plaster. The deafening bang instantly ceased everything. Silence filled the room.

"Lomax, I'm here to get you out!" Carver yelled.

The fighting had stopped. All the prisoners surrounding Scott stood stock still, like a video game on pause. Scott spat a mouth full of blood onto the floor and stood up straight.

"Then why didn't you just say so." Scott let go of an inmate he'd been holding up by the hair, dropping him to the floor in a crumpled pile, and casually walked over toward the open door. Carver followed a half step behind. As soon as they'd passed the threshold of the doorway, the guards pulled it shut, locking it instantly.

Scott walked along the corridor then stopped. A familiar smell of cheap cologne lingered in the air. One of the guards gave a recognizable sniff as he straightened up against the side of the wall.

Carver panicked for a moment, unsure of what was going to happen next.

Scott turned to face the guard with the nasal twitch. The one that delivered the message about Nathan when he was locked in solitary. The one who ignored him about protecting Nathan. Scott looked him dead in the eye. "I'm coming back for you!" He growled before turning and walking out. The guard stood still and gulped but said nothing.

After signing out his personal effects and going through the most rapid prison release in US history, Scott followed Carver to his car and sat in the passenger seat. Carver drove out of the parking lot back toward the city.

"I've got a chance for you to earn your freedom," Carver said.

"I was getting out next week anyway," Scott grunted.

"You're not up for parole," Carver said with a squint.

"Who said anything about parole?" Scott said with a laugh. "Why did you come for me?"

"There's a situation I need your help with." Carver sped along the bumpy road.

"Ha! The last time I helped you with a situation, I ended up with my ass in there!" Scott said, pointing his thumb back toward the prison.

"You killed three men getting me the name of one guy!" Carver snapped.

Speeding up, even more, leaving a dust trail behind him.

"You said it was urgent!"

"It was!" Carver shouted. "That one guy could have killed hundreds, if not thousands of citizens if we didn't stop him."

"Then it seems like you had a fair trade," Scott said, folding his arms.

"That's not the way it works." Carver put his foot down as his temper boiled.

"You knew what I was before you hired me!" Scott snapped.

"You still have to answer to the law."

"Oh, so the laws apply when it suits you? Use me when you need me, and put me back in my box when you're finished with me. You shouldn't have bothered. I'm not a weapon you can pull out when you need me and lock away again when you're done."

"This is different," Carver said.

"It always is," Scott replied cynically. He paused for thought for a few moments and took advantage of his situation. The leverage he'd just inadvertently obtained became more apparent. He wouldn't even be in this car right now if he didn't have some form of value or play some kind of pivotal role in whatever was going on. He decided he had a hand to play, even if he didn't know exactly what his hand was. "There's a kid in the infirmary back there. Name's Nathan. Get him out and to some place safe." Scott stated with a commanding tone.

"I'm not really sure that's even a possib—"

"It wasn't a question!" Scott gnashed before continuing. It was time to test the barrier. Time to get more of an idea of his current value. "If you want me to consider anything you're asking, then get this kid to safety." Scott changed his tone and carried on. "Now tell me about this situation you've got and why exactly you've gotten me into it."

"I'll make a call and get the kid taken care of," Carver mumbled as he capitulated.

Scott's mood changed as his test delivered results that exceeded his expectations. He obviously had a worth of which he'd not yet completely become aware. His incomplete thoughts were derailed as Carver continued.

"There's a guy who is going to kill ten thousand Americans if we don't give him what he wants," Carver told him. Calming himself down as, the bumps in the road smoothed out the closer they got to the main highway.

"Then give him what he wants," Scott answered with a cavalier tone of indifference.

"We can't. He has a way of remotely killing people. He's already killed the secretary of defense. He's even sent us the list of the people he's going to kill, he's that confident that nobody can stop him."

"Why should I care?" Scott asked.

"Here," Carver said, picking up a stack of paper from the foot well of the passenger side floor and throwing it into Scott's lap. "Here's the list."

"So?" Scott said, flicking through the pages aimlessly.

"Check out name sixty-one-twelve," Carver instructed him.

Scott fingered through the pages until he got to the one he needed. He slid his index finger down the paper until he got to sixty-one-twelve. He stopped. His world stopped. A look of fear and sheer panic filled his face. A terror consumed him as he'd never felt before.

Chapter 8

"Take me to him!" Scott ordered.

"He's in protective custody. Even if I knew where he was, we wouldn't be allowed access to see him." Carver looked at Scott, concerned about how he would react. If Scott didn't get some other way to get what he wanted, things would get nasty very quickly. He needed to think of a way to give Scott something else to focus on and fast. "Catching this man is the only way to stop this. Can you find him?"

"We wouldn't be having this conversation if you didn't think I could."

"We have less than forty-eight hours."

"Then you better get your foot down."

Carver raced to the FBI field office. Scott was rushed through a signing-in process and swiftly issued a set of "consultant" credentials. Soon after, Carver led Scott up the stairs bringing him up to speed as they ascended to the main room of operations.

"The guy's name's Raymond Napier. He's got Ph.Ds in advanced physics, human biology, medical chemistry, and more qualifications than I can even remember. He's a seriously clever cookie." Carver briefed Scott on the details offering everything they knew. "We've got teams of people trying to go through the list to find a commonality, but there's so many of them. It could take weeks before we even get close to finding the common denominator of these people. We've tracked Napier's movements through college, his travels to study in Germany, and only for a short time after he got back. The last record we've got has him making friends with a guy called Douglas Wilde. Napier picked him up the day he was released from prison, then he dropped off the grid. We've got nothing for the last four years." Carver opened the door as they reached the top of the stairs. "He's worked hard to stay off the grid. We've got guys looking at a ransom video he sent for anything they can find, but so far, they're coming up empty-handed."

"What about Wilde?" Scott asked.

"Pretty much the same. Went on a violent rampage. Killed a handful of people and hurt a bunch more. Got off with a lenient sentence due to his previous military service and a compelling presentation by a good lawyer of diminished responsibility." Carver said as they walked into the bustling ops room. "Wilde's a dangerous guy, a regular chart-topper on the Vicap system, teamed up with Napier, and I don't like where this could head."

A still of Raymond Napier had been printed onto photo paper and stuck up next to one of Douglas Wilde. The room was like a hive of activity buzzing away as Scott stood still, staring at the printouts. He looked at the pictures and information on the evidence board, carefully studying the photo of Napier first.

"High arch, almost triangular eyebrows." Was Scott's first observation.

"What?" Carver asked.

"Profiling people by facial features help you to get an idea of a personality type quickly and effectively if you know what to look for. People with high arch eyebrows are usually solid leaders. They love information and have the desire to be right but only based on the information they have. However, they will research the research and deconstruct the facts. They need to be in control and usually have a broad scope of expertise. Also, if you look at his proxemics ..."

"His what?" Carver asked with a frown.

"His proxemics. The distance between the eyebrow and the top of the eyelids." Scott watched as Carver nodded to indicate he now got it before continuing. "His are pretty high, indicating a reserved personality and a higher need for formalities. Usually preferring distance both physically and emotionally." Scott was about to voice more facts based on his observations from the pictures, but his attention was briefly captured by a beautiful brunette with a slim figure walking with purpose toward Carver. Carver spotted her as she approached and looked up with a smile. A gentle hint of Channel perfume accompanied Mary's presence.

"Ah, perfect," Carver said. "Scott, this is Mary Collins from Oxford University, England. She's an expert on all things medical. She'll be accompanying you to offer advice and assistance along the way."

"Very pleased to meet you. How do you do?" Mary said with the politest of English accents, followed by a smile and the smallest of knee bends, like some kind of an upright bow.

"Hell no! I work alone. And the last thing I need is Mary Poppins here, tagging along and slowing me down!" Scott said, spitting as he talked.

"It's Mary Collins!" Carver said abruptly.

"Oh, I see, that's how we're going to start things off, are we?" Mary said with the slightest of frowns displayed on her forehead.

"No offense, but you'll get in the way and probably end up getting hurt or worse if I have to take you with me. I'm sure Carver can find something else useful for you to do. Maybe watch the kids." Scott finished with a contemptuous one-sided smile.

Carver pulled Scott aside. Mary watched as the two men turned away, and Carver spoke to Scott quietly.

"Hey, she's got a name on that list, too. Do what you have to. Just work with her, she's more useful than she looks, believe me."

Scott straightened up and took in a deep breath before blowing out a long sigh. He looked over at her and back at Carver. He knew Carver was going to insist. And it wouldn't hurt to have a little eye candy with him. She was definitely a head-turner. *She might even be good to use as a distraction*, Scott thought, convincing himself of the positive reasons to agree.

"Okay, but if anything happens to her …" Scott was interrupted.

"I can assure you that I will be perfectly fine," Mary said sharply. "I'm quite capable of looking after myself should the need arise."

Scott and Carver both smiled before turning back to the task at hand. Carver shuffled through scattered papers and piled up files on the desktop. Scott looked over at the evidence wall again. He focused on one particular photo.

"Tell me what we know about the death of the secretary of defense," Scott said, looking over at Carver and Mary.

Mary jumped in first. "We don't know much. He was at a secure location. Surrounded by Secret Service personnel." She was about to continue when Scott cut in.

"No, not that. What actually killed him?" Scott asked.

"Well, we don't know. He had a kind of fit and died on the spot." Mary stated, not sure where Scott was going with this.

"Heart stopped?" Lomax asked.

"The M.E. put "Cause of death unknown" on the certificate. One very unusual thing, though," Mary said as her mind worked back to recall the details.

"Now we're getting somewhere," Scott mumbled under his breath.

"The autopsy showed something impossibly weird."

"What was that?"

"Post-mortem reports showed that there were no red blood cells in his body. Not a single one. Like they'd all vanished instantly. Which is impossible, of course. Without red blood cells, oxygen cannot be delivered through the blood to the muscle, brain, vital organs, or any other part of the body." There a hint of annoyance in Mary's voice that the anomaly couldn't be explained.

"Get me everything you can on deaths with similar attributes," Scott commanded.

"Do you ever say please?" Mary asked sarcastically with a teasing smile.

"Only when I'm in a good mood," Scott replied.

"Oh, and when's that?" she asked.

"Don't know yet. I'm still waiting for it to happen." Scott grunted.

"Here, I've got something," Carver said, jabbing away at keys on the computer in front of him and pulling the information up on the huge display screen in front of them all. "A series of unexplained deaths with the exact same post-mortem results. The most recent, Lucy Frampton, wife of billionaire Neil

Frampton, CEO of VICI Pharmaceuticals, died within a couple of days of hiring a K&R negotiator and the family nanny. All died from sudden unexplained death, and autopsy results showing absolutely no red bloods cells in the body post-mortem."

"Looks like we've got a thread," Scott said. "Can you take me to pick up my car and some personal effects I'm going to need?"

"Sure, let's go," Carver said, grabbing his jacket.

"Oh lovely, a field trip. I'll get my purse," Mary said with a smile, her face filled with an expression of enthusiasm. Scott just flashed an exasperated look at Carver.

Scott followed Carver to the parking lot, with Mary trailing along eagerly a half step behind. Carver started the car with Mary sitting behind him. Scott sat shotgun and looked at Mary as she pulled her cell phone from her purse.

"I'm just going to call Darcy, the next-door neighbor. I need to get her to feed my cat." Mary said politely as she put the phone to her ear.

Scott analyzed her statement. *My* cat, instead of; *the* cat. That means she's more than likely single. He knew from experience that people in relationships or who were married mostly used the term *the* cat, *the* bed, *the* bedroom, etc. Whereas single people usually say *my* cat, *my* bed, *my* bedroom, and so on. The word *my* also denoted possession and closeness. So when Mary said "the" next-door neighbor instead of "my" next-door neighbor, it highlighted to him that although they got along, it wasn't an extremely close relationship. Close enough to ask a favor here and there, but that was about it. Scott was starting to build a mental profile up of his new partner.

Some habits die hard, Scott thought to himself as he listened to her quick phone conversation, his analytical mind whirring away, instantly concluding masses of calculations as he made mental notes about Mary, building up a picture in his mind about who she really was.

After ending the call, she became engrossed in her phone. Scott continued to observe discreetly as he gave directions.

"Remember what I briefed you on this morning," Carver said, looking into the rearview mirror to see if Mary was paying attention. She quickly looked up with a slight head shake and focused on what was happening around her again.

"Sorry, I was having a text conversation about what was going on here with my brother," Mary responded.

Yet again, Scott noticed her sentence structure. People always put their priorities in order. The fact that she talked about the situation with her brother could mean that she was prioritizing what she was in the middle of. On the other hand, it could also mean that her brother was not her top priority in her life, or at the moment, there was some distance between them. It also revealed that as Carver hadn't said anything about her text conversation with her brother, it was highly likely that it was her brother who was the one on the list and also in protective custody. Mid-thought, Scott had another revelation. None of this was unexpected. She'd been briefed. She'd been tasked. She knew what was coming and what was expected of her. Carver had given her a full run down. Mary wasn't there to a partner. She was there to be a leash!

Well, what she might think could be as easy as walking a dog on a lead in the park, could end up being one hell of a rodeo! I hope she's prepared, Scott thought.

Less than a twenty-minute drive with Scott giving directions had them pulling up at a house in a reasonable neighborhood. It was pretty run down in comparison to the other houses in the area but had the potential to be a nice home.

"Wait here," Scott said, alighting the car and walking up the path toward the front door. Before he was halfway, the door had already started to open. A young lady stood there watching as Scott approached.

"He's not here." The lady's voice called, not saying who exactly she was referring to.

"I know," Scott answered as he continued to walk toward the door.

Brandi was only a couple of hoop earrings and a tattoo away from what most people would consider trailer trash. But she had a good heart and was as honest as the day is long. That was one of the reasons Scott had given her his house. But not the main reason. The main reason was a lot more of an important aspect of Scott's life. Having blown up many bridges in his life, Scott had a shortage of friends and reliable acquaintances. Like it or not, Brandi was one of the very few people Scott could truly trust.

"I'm just here to pick up my car and some bits and pieces."

Brandi reached in behind the door and took a set of keys off the hook.

"Car's in the garage." She tossed him the keys. "And all of your personal stuff's in the back packed up in trunks." She stepped aside, fully opening the door. Scott placed his hands on either side of her pulling her into him for a hug and giving her a friendly kiss on the cheek.

"Thanks, Brandi," he said, walking into the house.

Brandi closed the door behind him as she closely eyed the occupants of the car waiting outside. Within a few minutes, Scott had gathered up the kit he wanted and the electronic door of the garage started to rise open.

The engine of the metallic gun metal gray Porsche Cayenne grumbled as he slowly pulled forward. The smell of the huge new rubber tires filled the air as they squeaked along the garage's painted floor. Followed by the waft of exhaust fumes as he edged it out onto the drive. He lowered the electric window, looking over to Mary, who was still patiently waiting in Carver's car.

"Come on, let's go pull that thread," Scott shouted.

Mary jumped into the Porsche with Scott, immediately appreciating the sumptuous leather interior and luxurious refineries the prestigious car had to offer.

"A big Porsche Cayenne, huh? What are you compensating for?" Mary asked, deliberately testing Scott.

"Not having a very big … family!" He replied without reaction. He pulled away and drove toward the address they had on file for Neil Frampton.

It wasn't long before they pulled up outside a modest condo. Neil was playing out the front with his children. He was a shadow of his former self. His impeccable suit changed for casual attire. His polished exterior and manicured appearance were now humbled. A short beard had replaced his clean-shaven look, and his trimmed hair was now overgrown. The color of his skin had even seemed to change, and he looked somewhat drained.

Scott stepped out of the car, with Mary cautiously following his lead. The temperature seemed to have decreased with a cloud looming above, adding an almost gray feeling to the part of town they'd arrived in.

"Neil?" Scott asked as he approached. "Neil Frampton?"

"Go on inside, kids," Neil instructed, and they immediately complied, picking up the ball as they did. "I don't want to talk to anyone." He looked up as Scott neared him, Mary a couple of steps behind.

"I just want to ask you a few questions," Scott said calmly.

"I told you. I don't want to talk to anyone!" Neil snapped, watching Scott.

Scott stopped. He saw a look in Neil's eyes that was way too familiar. A look Scott knew only too well.

Chapter 9

Scott took a moment to calculate what he should do next. He observed Neil was living with pain and guilt that couldn't be explained to anyone or understood by a soul except for those who'd been through it. A deeply carved grief line ran down the middle of his eyes from the bottom of his forehead to the top of his nose. More grief lines ran around his lips, accompanied by signs of stress demonstrated by the tops of his eyelids sagging low. Scott took it all in as he stared at Neil. The first thing he knew; Neil didn't kill his wife. That was for sure. The second thing; his kids were everything he had left in his world. And the final observation; something terrified Neil more than death itself.

"We'll be out of your way in no time, Mr. Frampton," Scott said in an attempt to reassure Neil that it would be okay.

"Are you a cop?" Neil asked.

"No. I'm just looking for someone, and I think you can help me. I need to talk to you about what happened to your wife." Scott spoke as softly as he could.

Neil's eyes filled with fear, his mouth opening involuntarily. A visible display of panic showed, and the last remaining shade of color drained from his face.

"I don't know anything. I don't want to talk about it. He knows everything. He can kill anybody. Like that!" Neil snapped his fingers. "I don't want to get involved. He knows everything I do." Neil backed away toward his front door. "I'm not risking it.

I'm not getting involved." Neil turned and ran inside his house. The sound of the door being bolted from the inside could be heard as Scott turned to walk back to the Porsche.

"Aren't you going to knock? Try and find out more?" Mary asked.

"That man's been through enough," Scott said quietly, speaking from his throat. "Something's frightened him. Frightened him more than I ever could. He wouldn't say anything if I beat him from here to his grave. Let's go."

"Where are we going?" Mary followed with growing curiosity.

"To find out the root of his torment," Scott said, climbing into the Porsche.

The weather improved as they drove to the other side of town. The day got brighter and warmer as they discreetly penetrated into the classy end of town, where even the pooches get their own stylists. The Porsche engine growled as they pulled into millionaire's row, driving along the palatial houses of the rich and spoiled. A couple of minutes in and they slowed to a stop outside Neil Frampton's former home. It was now empty but still managed to look impeccably magnificent.

"Wow, that's quite the house," Mary said as they pulled into the driveway.

"Let's just have a look around, see if we can see anything out of the ordinary," Scott said, switching off the car's engine.

They alighted the car and walked up the pathway toward the main entrance. The brilliant white exterior of the huge house almost glowed in the reflected sunlight. Birds sang in the trees at the perimeter of the house grounds, and the smell of the array of the previous owner's choices filled the air from the flowerbeds under each window.

"You go that way, and I'll go this way," Scott said, indicating they should both take different directions around the outside of the house.

"What are we looking for?" Mary asked.

"I don't know yet. I'm hoping we'll know when we see it."

Mary seemed to accept his answer and slowly began to skirt around the house, examining all she could see but not really sure what exactly she was meant to be looking for. She'd only moved a few paces when she heard something make a banging noise, followed by the sound of crunching wood. She looked around to see the front door had been kicked in.

Scott stood there, inches from the splintered wood. "Oh look, it's open," he said with a sheepish smile.

"What are you doing? That's breaking and entering. We're on private property and could get into trouble. We can't go in there."

"Sure we can," Scott reassured her casually, making a gesture with his hand to indicate she could go first. "You've got permission to go anywhere you want."

"I do?" she asked, stepping through the doorway.

"Of course."

"And who granted this permission?" she asked.

"Me!" he said, following her inside. "See what you can find." Scott wandered off into the depths of the house. Mary stifled her frustration as she walked around to see whatever it was they were now looking for on the inside. Meanwhile, Scott tried to visualize what each room was used for and where the furniture would have been. He worked his way around, trying to picture the layout of each room and what purpose it would have served.

In each room, he decided from tell-tale signs what function it filled. Indentations in the carpet showed the position of the desk in the center of what he had deduced was the study. Worn carpet behind it was once home to a swivel chair and confirmed his thoughts. The wall opposite the window had dark spots, where the sun-bleached wallpaper had housed what he presumed would have been a notice board, with wall calendars and year planners on either side. Wall lights sat on either side of a gap where a family portrait had once sat in Scott's estimations. His eyes traced the wall upwards to the air conditioning vent, directly opposite where the desk would have been. A slight gut feeling drew him closer to it. He wasn't sure what it was yet, but something didn't seem right.

He stretched to get a closer look. There it was. Scratches showing the bare brass in and around the screws that were previously covered in the white paint that had furnished the trim in the rest of the room. They weren't new, but they were more recent than the last time the room had been decorated. Somebody had unscrewed the vent in the office of Neil Frampton before the attack on his family.

Scott curled his fingers around the top of the vent cover. One powerful pull, and he ripped the cover away from the ventilation shaft. And there it was. Confirmation of Scott's suspicion. He carefully extracted it with a his thumb and forefinger.

"And now we have our next thread," Scott whispered under his breath.

Chapter 10

Scott slipped the small electronic device into his pocket and exited the room. He paced toward the front door. It was time to get out of there before the local cops arrived. It was time to start pulling on the next thread.

"Come on, time to go," he shouted to Mary.

"Where are we going?" she asked.

"Radio Shack," Scott replied.

"Do they still even exist?" Mary asked.

"Something similar will, that's for sure."

They jumped back in the Porsche and sped away toward the busy downtown streets. Scott scanned the shops until eventually he spotted

something that might point him in the
right direction. A small independent
gadget shop. The window was filled with
mobile phones, tablets, and imported
Chinese electronic devices. He pulled
the Porsche into a parking spot nose
first and hopped out. He was in the shop
before Mary had even managed to get
out of the car.

Scott marched up to the glass-top
counter filled with memory cards, cell
phone covers, and charging leads. He
pulled the device out of his pocket and
held it up to the spotty-faced kid behind
the counter.

"Where can I buy these?" Scott
asked.

The kid looked concerned why
the huge man was aggressively asking
questions. Slightly frightened of the
extremely forward approach, the kid

looked up at Mary, like a child looking to a parent for permission to speak.

"It's quite all right," Mary said. "He just lacks some basic manners sometimes. He won't hurt you."

"I might." Scott growled, feeling the decision should be his as to who may or may not get hurt and who gets to do it. Mary, who was still a step behind Scott, shook her head, and the kid focused on the device.

"Not the kind of thing we do here. Try Tac-Tronics. That's the kind of stuff they sell." The kid looked between Scott and Mary.

A quick internet search and a ten-minute drive had them at a retail park looking at the shop front for Tac-Tronics.

Tac-Tronics – Tactical electronic equipment for all your needs.

The store had all the hallmarks to show it was previously a pawn shop. Scott parked a good distance away, taking everything in on the short walk back to the store. Sandwiched between a new budget clothes shop to the left called The Emperor's, which was the last shop in the row, and Delilah's Hairdressers to the right. After that was Golden Shower Chinese takeaway, Shampooch Dog Groomers sat in the corner spot before the L shape array of shops continued with V. Lustig Sales Training and Hot and Ready Pizza Shop, which was home to a worn sign pointing to Oswald's target training down a track to the rear. Tac-Tronics didn't seem anything particularly special at first glance.

Scott tried the door, hoping what was on the inside was going to be more promising than the flaky ill-maintained exterior offered. A buzzer sounded as he entered the under-lit shop. Dark blue carpet tiles, covered with stains looked like they hadn't been replaced since the shop was built, provided a walkway between a row of glass cabinets displaying spy gear on his right and an L-shaped counter with bars going up to the ceiling ran down the other side and back wall of the small store. A steel door with a pin pad to the right rear looked like it had seen better days but was still solid enough, and shelves of circuit boards and boxes of electronic components filled the wall behind the counter.

"How can I help you?" a voice asked from the rear of the shop. Not looking up straight away as he shoved a bunch of stuff in a drawer, like a kid hiding a porn mag, when his mom walks into his room.

"Do you know who sells these?" Scott asked, showing him the device.

"I never seen that kind of thing before." He answered too quickly for Scott's liking. "I don't sell anything like that."

The guy hadn't even taken it into his hands to examine it. He wasn't even close to the counter. Not close enough to get a good look anyway. When someone presents you with something new that you don't recognize in a field you work in, curiosity alone is usually enough to get you to reach out and take hold of whatever it is in question. This guy was too dismissive. He knew exactly what it was and where it came from.

Scott did a second scan of the shop. He could probably kick his way through the wooden panels beneath the counter, but they might also be secured at the rear. Even if they weren't, this guy could probably be out and gone before Scott managed to get through the wood. He looked up, hoping for ceiling tiles, but it was a solid ceiling. A false ceiling might have meant he could have gone over the bars. The steel door was definitely the strongest part of the setup.

"Okay, thanks for your help." Scott turned to walk out, much to Mary's surprise. Scott paid close attention to the inside of the shop's door as he left. Two bolts, top, and bottom. A mortice lock with signs of use at the center. The usual cylinder locks in the door that turned from the inside, and an electronic lock released by the buzzer from behind the counter with a manual override. When he opened the door, he looked outside. Only one mortice lock keyhole.

The one he'd probably lock if he nipped out for a few minutes to grab lunch, Scott thought. The electronic roller shutters were probably controlled by a switch on the other side of the counter. No alarm pin pad by the front door to arm it as he left.

Mary followed closely, closing the door behind her as she tagged along back to the Porsche.

"That's it? We're just going to give up?" she asked.

"Nope," Scott replied, climbing into the Porsche and firing up the engine to get the AC running. "We just need to approach from a different angle." Scott had figured the shopkeeper locked his doors from the inside and left through the back door at closing time. He pulled the car over to the fast food drive-through. He ordered meals and drinks for both of them, then used the exit to allow him to turn left and slip off the parking lot, and around the corner, into the service road that ran the length of the rear of the retail park.

Stopping about four or five hundred yards back from the rear door of Tac-Tronics, Scott pulled the car over and switched off the engine.

"Now what?" Mary asked.

"Now we wait," Scott said, unwrapping his burger. Both of them tucked in and kept an eye out for movement at the back of the shop.

"Wait for what?" Mary asked, slipping a handful of fries from the box.

"Wait until I can get a hold of him and make him tell me the truth," Scott replied, taking a second bite of his burger.

"What makes you think he was lying?"

"His blink rate went sky high when I showed him the device, followed by a one-sided shoulder shrug as he answered. He saw the device but was looking at me and locked eye contact the entire time he spewed out his answer."

"I thought if someone kept eye contact when they answered you, it was a sign of them telling the truth."

"Most people do. Eye contact is usually good, but not prolonged eye contact. It's actually a sign of deception. People telling the truth will give eye contact and look away in proportionate amounts. If someone's lying to you, they tend to hold the eye contact. It sounds counter-intuitive, but the reason is; they want to keep watching closely to see how you respond to their lie. They want to get a read on whether you believe them or not, so they watch closely to how you react."

"Okay, that makes sense, I suppose," Mary said with a nod as she slipped another couple of fries into her mouth.

Without the air conditioning running, it didn't take too long for the interior of the car to start heating up in the summer sun. Mary was starting to feel the heat, fanning herself while Scott stayed focused on the rear door of the shop. He told her the rest of his reasons for believing the shopkeeper was lying to him as they finished their meals and explained that's why he wanted to catch him off guard and get the upper hand.

There was movement. Scott slotted his drink into the cup holder. The door of the shop was pushed open, and before Mary had even realized it, Scott was out of the car.

"What are you going to do?" Mary asked with a finishing slurp on her drink and giving it a little shake that rattled the remaining ice at the bottom.

"Ask him some questions," Scott replied before he ran the length of the service road toward the shopkeeper at an incredible speed. Mary hated to admit it to herself, but she was impressed by how fast this huge guy could move when he did. She watched with fascination as Scott bolted toward the shopkeeper.

The shopkeeper was oblivious to Scott thundering toward him like a football player about to tackle. He slowly closed the door over like he'd done countless times before and selected the key he wanted to lock the rear door.

Scott held his forearm out in front of him, like a truck bumper, as he neared the shopkeeper. Still at full pace, he pounded into him, sending the shopkeeper and himself crashing into the steel security door at the rear of the shop. Winded, dazed, and confused, the shopkeeper crumpled to the floor as Scott delivered the first kick to the guts.

Scott was unaware of Mary, rapidly approaching from behind as he continued to dish out kick after kick to the shopkeeper. Working his way up from the shopkeeper's lunch to the first of his ribs, Scott kept kicking.

"I thought you were just going to ask him a few questions?" Mary shouted.

"I haven't thought of any yet!" Scott shouted back, still kicking away.

"Well, don't you think you should? While he still has the ability to answer them!"

"Yeah, you're right," Scott said but continued to kick.

"Well?"

"I'm trying to think of a good one!" Scott yelled, still kicking the shopkeeper.

Scott stopped kicking and bent over to bring himself down to the groaning shopkeeper.

"Tell me about this!" Scott said, thrusting the device from Neil's house in front of the shopkeeper's face.

"That's a good question?" Mary asked but was unheard.

"It's not from me! I don't sell that kind of thing!" the shopkeeper cried.

"Then where did it come from?" Scott growled, getting angrier, but his anger suddenly subsided. Everything changed when he heard the shopkeeper's reply.

"I can't sell anything like that. It's government issue."

Chapter 11

Scott held the shopkeeper's hair at the top of his scalp to keep him in place while he slipped the device back into his pocket. He thought about what the shopkeeper had told him.

"So, who would I see if I wanted to buy something like this?" Scott asked.

"I don't know," the shopkeeper replied.

"Think!" Scott shouted, smashing the shopkeeper's head against the steel door.

"Okay, okay. Er, Al's."

"What?" Scott asked.

"Big Al's Diner in Elmont Ridge. Big Al's the guy to see to buy that kind of stuff."

Scott stood and kicked the shopkeeper again.

"It's true! I swear!" the shopkeeper yelled, bringing his arms up in front of him, trying to defend himself against Scott's blows.

"I think he's telling the truth," Mary said.

"I know," Scott replied. "This bit's just for fun."

Mary walked toward the Porsche, and a few kicks later, Scott joined her, sitting in the driver's seat and starting the engine. Mary had already pulled Big Al's Diner up on her smartphone.

"Head south." She pulled on her seatbelt.

Scott pulled away and started toward Big Al's.

"You don't seem too phased by violence." Scott looked over at Mary, who was deep in thought.

"I'm from London. Just because I'm polite enough to say 'Ooops, pardon me' and 'Cheerio' doesn't mean I'm not cold enough to cut your throat with a razor while you sleep. Believe me, I've seen and done it all. England banned guns, not violence."

Scott smiled, which turned to a snigger as he thought, *there's something about Mary!* He wasn't sure what it was, the icy yet beautiful exterior or the hidden vulnerable side that she kept locked away.

Mary gave directions all the way to Big Al's. As they pulled onto the parking lot, Scott spotted three cars to his immediate left. The deep dips in the ground of the three neighboring spaces indicated they were the regularly used parking spots of the staff. The three spaces were the ones that were in constant use as opposed to the other spaces where customers came and went and didn't show the same tell-tale signs of such continual use.

The first parking space as filled with a beat-up old Chevy. Stick figure decals on the rear window indicated the driver was a single mother of four with a dog. Judging by the condition, the car was having as much of a hard time coping with the four kids as the mother was.

The next car was a Taurus that looked like it had seen better days, too. A bumper sticker informed Scott the owner was a "Proud Navy Wife." Husband away for long periods of time. Never a great thing to advertise, in

Scott's opinion. A window sticker also made a point of showing off to the world her son was a star student at Black Valley High School.

The third car was the biggest alarm bell however. It was a shiny black Cadillac Escalade sitting in pride of place outside the diner. The license plate read BIG AL. It was days old, not months. Top of the range and way above the budget earned from the owner of a modest diner. It clearly stated Al was doing well off his nefarious dealings, but it looked like his staff weren't reaping the rewards as readily as he was. A few other average cars peppered the parking lot but nothing that stood out.

Scott parked and got out the Porsche. The contrast of the temperature outside when he opened the car door was almost the equivalent of opening an oven as he stepped out of the Porsche's cool air-conditioned cabin. He bounded toward the diner like he was on a mission. There was a time to gently probe and ask questions politely, and there was a time to go in *all guns blazing*, and this was the latter. Whoever Big Al was, at best, he was a thief or someone who sold stolen goods. At worst, he was a traitor. Either way, Scott was about to deliver a gift from inter-karma.

A bell above the door clinked more than rang as Scott walked in. The smell of smoked bacon and fried onions was collaborating with filter coffee to fill the room with an invisible hint of rising cholesterol levels. The extractor fans were losing the ongoing battle and almost ready to surrender. A lady with

Kacey on her nametag was about to ask if he'd like a table when Scott spotted a set of Ford keys with the name Emma on one of the fobs hanging behind the counter.

Making an educated guess, Scott leaned in to talk in a low but firm tone. "Tell Emma her husband's away and her son is being held at Black Valley High School. He'll be killed if any of you interfere. Now stay out of the way, and we'll let him go!" Scott growled as he walked past her. A look of terror filled the woman's face as she scurried off to find her colleague. Mary turned to the right and sat at a table quietly while Scott marched the opposite way and bounded around the rear of the counter.

Big Al was certainly that. The walking eclipse was a giant. He stood there at the hot plate flipping burgers, but it wasn't all muscle. He looked like he spent as much time eating as he did frying the food. Mary sat at her table discreetly and was pretending to read the menu. Scott wasn't that subtle.

"Two questions!" Scott roared, throwing the device onto the hotplate. "Who did you buy these off? And who did you sell them to?"

Big Al stood there temporarily dumbfounded. The shock of someone having the nerve to confront him like this was a rarity. It threw him off balance. For a moment, he thought it was a joke or maybe even a misunderstanding. Then he realized the mean-looking guy in front of him demanding answers wasn't messing around.

Scott saw Al's eyes move before his hand. He watched as Al looked at the carving knife and weighed up his options. Before Al could completely move his arm out to grab it, Scott reached in and bent his elbow. Al had managed to grip the knife, but Scott twisted his arm around. Al's strength was just enough to hold Scott back from pushing the blade into his gut, but Scott jumped up, launching his entire body weight upward and ramming his knee into the rear of the handle, thrusting the knife forward and into Al's stomach. It wasn't enough to kill him but certainly enough to do some damage. The knife dropped to the floor, and Scott took the opportunity to smash a right hook into Al's face. Another rapid jab, this time into Al's stomach, caused a squirt of blood to spray from Al's injury and was enough to fill Al with fear.

Scott recognized the moment of Al's mental submission. He slammed Al's head onto the hotplate.

"Where did you get them?" he shouted again.

The hotplate hissed as Al's face burned. He jumped back in pain. Scott used the momentum and smashed him into the milkshake machine directly behind him.

"Who did you sell them to?" Scott moved forward along the counter to smash Al's head into the cake chiller, but something caught his attention through the corner of his eye.

A cop car had pulled up, and two uniformed officers were entering the diner to take their break. Scott swiped the device and grabbed the car keys out of his pocket with his right hand, and grabbed Al's hair at the scalp with his left. Scott dragged him around the front of the counter and, using the panic and confusion of the customers as a shield, dropped the device and keys into Mary's lap, who was still sitting at one of the tables near the window. Scott pushed back hard and rammed Al into the counter.

"We haven't got long, so you better tell me quickly. Who did you sell these to?" Scott looked at Al, but there was no answer. He reached to his right and grabbed a glass bottle, smashing it over Al's head and holding it in a threatening way under his throat. "Who?"

It was too late. The police officers had entered the diner and seen Scott holding Al over the counter. Scott stood up and faced the officers. Al dropped to the floor behind him.

"It's not what it looks like," Scott said calmly, the broken bottle dropping from his hand.

"Turn around, get on your knees and place your hands above your head!" The first officer shouted in a state of controlled aggression. The way he'd obviously practiced so many times before.

"Okay," Scott said slowly, raising his hands and being compliant. "But I got to tell you I'm armed, I have a pistol in the rear waistband of my jeans."

The two officers both drew their weapons.

"On your knees!" the one shouted.

"Hands above your head!" the other yelled, both pointing their guns at Scott.

"Okay, I am. There's no need to get nasty. I was telling you I'm armed out of courtesy. I have no intention of using it." Scott lowered himself to his knees.

There was no two ways about it, Scott could have taken both of them out and then gone back to finish what he started with Al. He thought to himself as the one officer clicked the first bracelet of the cuffs onto his wrist. Was he going to injure or kill a couple of cops for just doing their job, though? Of course not. It's not like they were a corrupt prison officer racket, profiting from gangs inside the detention center he just came from. In Scott's mind, they were scum. It had taken him a while to learn the good from the bad. The ones who participated from the ones who just turned a blind eye. They were all as bad as each other. Half of them were smuggling drugs into the prison for an extra income and were just as corrupt as most of the inmates.

Scott felt the cold steel of the second bracelet tighten around his wrist and stood up. The slightest of side-to-side head movements indicated to Mary not to get involved. The one cop led Scott out to the car, and the other called dispatch for an ambulance for Big Al. Scott was in a world of shit now. The clock was ticking. And he needed to find the man that could bring all of this to an end.

Chapter 12

Scott had been booked in, processed, and locked in a cell at the local sheriff's office with haste and efficiency. He'd taken in every tiny detail he could during the process. Window fixings and locations, exits, alarm systems, CCTV, number of personnel working. Anything he could make a point of observing while he had the chance. Anything that might come in handy to know if he had to make his own way out. They'd bagged and tagged his gear and graced him with a pillow and blanket before closing the heavy steel cell door shut, ready for what was expected to be a long wait.

The cell had that smell that Scott was so used to. The similar smell they all shared. A little like the dusty school storage rooms that held the gym equipment.

Scott's thoughts went down the path of the device being government issue and the possible ways it had come to be in the possession of a café owner. Then, how many hands it would have gone through before it ended up in Neil Frampton's house. More and more possibilities of what was happening opened up as he lay there with his thoughts.

Lomax decided to break things down in his head, starting with what he knew. Carver may have been the guy who showed up to get him out but even as an FBI SAC, he would have needed authorization to get him out. Which means the permission had come from much higher up. Taking what Carver had told him into consideration, the links in the chain could go as high up as the White House. After all, it's not just the potential victims here but the murder of the SECDEF. At this stage, the limited information he had wouldn't give him the answers he wanted, but he would certainly keep in mind the possibility of how high this whole thing could stretch.

There was one hell of a gap between the White House and a greasy diner, and Lomax had every intention of closing that gap. First, though, he had to confirm for sure that the two were linked.

He could still smell the grease on him from the diner, and a waft of burned skin from when he slammed Al's face onto the hotplate lingered in his nostrils. He blew it out as he laughed at the irony of being out of prison less than a day and getting himself locked up again.

Thoughts of Mary drifted into Lomax's mind. An enthusiastic look in her eye when it first came to light they were leaving the office. Then again, when he called her to get into his car. Like that of an eager puppy. A look almost of excitement. Similar to a child being told they can go on the car ride they'd been pestering their parent to come on when the parent finally concedes. It appeared she didn't get out much. Very much like himself. Something that needed to change and quickly.

If something didn't happen soon, he'd have to look at how he was going to escape. It wouldn't be too hard, he could simply tie his shirt sleeve around his neck, secure the other sleeve somewhere at the top of the cell door and give it a kick. The clang would echo and grab the attention of the deputy. Lomax would give the impression he's swinging there as he made a few choking sounds then, when the deputy opened the cell door, Lomax would make his move. Relieve the deputy of his pistol and use him as a human shield to get him to the next stage. He couldn't stay here for too much longer. He had a job to do. Before he had come close to formulating a plan, footsteps approached, and his cell door shot open.

"I don't know who you are or who you know, but they must be some pretty powerful people. Orders came down right from the top." The deputy didn't keep eye contact with Scott for long. "We're to let you go without charge, give you back your gun and belongings, help you in any way we can and do anything you tell us to."

"Well fuck me," Scott whispered under his breath as he swung his legs over the edge of the bed and sat up. He glanced at the deputy, who was standing there sheepishly. "Anything?" he asked, an eyebrow cocked.

"Anything!" The deputy affirmed with a submissive look downward, giving the impression he'd already been scorned that day in relation to what was going on.

After grabbing his gear and making a couple of quick phone calls to find out where Mary and his car were, it was time to go. He was starting to appreciate how Mary was handling things. Grateful for her resilience and lack of squeamish tendencies.

Maybe I was a little rough on her at first, he thought to himself.

He stared at the deputy and smiled. "Time to go," Scott said happy with the recent turn of events and assuming Carver had helped him out of this sticky situation somehow. After all, it was Carver who got him out of prison, Scott reasoned.

Scott raced the police cruiser out of the station's secure car park and skidded it onto the road. The deputy sat in the passenger seat clinging on for dear life as Scott jumped the V8 Crown Vic over a hump in the road. Sirens blazing and lights flashing, Scott rocketed down the street.

"Yeeee-ha!" he shouted as he swung a left, the tires screeching and the deputy turning white. "This is fun. I got to get me one of these things. Look at how all the people just courteously move out of the way."

"You done high-speed chase driving before?" the deputy asked.

"Oh yeah!" Scott answered. "Just never in a squad car."

"What do you normally drive?"

"The car in front!" Scott answered, this time swinging a right. They made it to Mary's townhouse in record time. He spotted his Porsche from the end of the street and pulled up outside. To the deputy's relief, Scott got out of the car and banged the roof a couple of times.

"Thanks for all your help, Officer. You can get out of here now," Scott said, walking up the path toward the front door. The deputy scrambled to get into the driver's seat and away before Scott had chance to change his mind.

Scott approached Mary's house taking in all he could as he got closer. He spotted a customized steel access ramp on the floor. He tried the front door, but it was locked, so he knocked a couple of times, but there was no answer. He walked down the side alley and reached over the gate. Feeling around, he located the bolt and pulled it back, pressed the latch, and the gate opened. He locked it back up behind him and strolled to the rear of the house. The outward opening steel screen door was locked. He scanned the rear garden until he spotted what he was looking for. One of the plants had a pliable wire rod to help support it as it grew. Scott plucked it from its home and bent it into a hook shape.

A couple of attempts was all it took before he got the shape right and was able to feed it between the small gaps of the metal screen door and around to reach the rear of the doorknob. A little twist and the lock was undone from the inside. He turned the knob and opened the door a fraction, then slipped the wire back out. Scott straightened it out again and slid it back into its home among the plant life. He turned the knob on the inner door. As he suspected, it was unlocked. He quietly slipped inside. Nobody was in the room. He controlled his breathing and, without a sound, turned on the spot, slowly closing and re-locking the outer door and, almost silently, steadying the inner door back to being completely closed until he'd clicked it shut.

The sound of water running from upstairs told Scott that Mary was in the shower. An elusive smell similar to dollar tree furniture polish, mixed with bookstore and potpourri, lingered lightly around him. He took his time and moved slowly and quietly as he looked around the living room. Trophies for gymnastics were all over the place. Photos of Mary from a young age, growing through the years in different poses at professional gymnastic tournaments. More photos of a young boy clearly suffering from some kind of disability. Too old to be her child, especially in some of the pictures of them together. More than likely a sibling. Framed pictures of her parents through the years but nothing recent. Nothing from the last six or seven years. Around the same time as the last dates on the trophies and the pictures at the gymnastics competitions stopped. Scott's best guess was that her parents had passed away and left her to look after her sick brother.

The tall bookcase at the rear of the room was crammed with books on diseases and medical studies. An access door leading to a cupboard under the stairs separated the bookcase and a desk littered with paperwork and case studies from a university and letters from medical professionals. Unpaid medical bills piled up among folders of project work. The noise from the shower stopped.

Mary hurriedly came down the stairs soaking wet in nothing other than a small white towel wrapped around her. She turned to grab something and jumped in shock, seeing Scott in her house. A sharp intake of breath, and the pupils of her eyes dilated as she looked up at him in a moment of fear.

"How did you get in here?" she asked in a state of panic.

"Quietly," he said.

"Well, I hope you haven't damaged anything."

"Not yet," Scott said with a smile, eyeing her up and down as she stood dripping wet in a towel. "Hurry up, we've got work to do. I got to get back and finish off hurting Big Al."

Mary left whatever it was she came down the stairs to grab and scurried back up to get dried and dressed. She left the bedroom door open so she could shout down to Scott below.

"No need. While you were locked up, I followed Al to the hospital. You did quite the number on him. He was more than delicate, shall we say, by the time I got to him." Mary pulled on a pair of tight jeans and slipped a crop top over her head.

"Good, so he was already softened up for you. How many times did you have to whack him before he talked?" Scott shouted back up the stairs as he wandered into the open-plan kitchen area.

"I didn't," Mary stated. "You don't always have to use violence, you know."

"I know, I just like to." Scott laughed, pulling the fridge door open. He took a plate of something out and peeled back the clear plastic wrap. A quick sniff of whatever it was, had him quickly slipping it back onto the shelf it came from.

"I told him the urgency of what we needed to know and one or two other things, and he told me what I wanted to know." She pulled a black boot over her jeans and zipped it up to the knee.

"Just like that?" Scott asked dubiously, considering her sentence structure.

"Pretty much," Mary replied, pulling on the second boot.

"You just told him it was important, and he spilled the beans?" Scott shouted up as he took a chicken leg out of a container and gave it a quick sniff. Satisfied it was edible, he took a bite and closed the fridge door.

"Well, mostly. I told him a couple of other things, too, and he gave me exactly what I wanted." Mary grabbed a small black leather jacket from the wardrobe along with her purse and began to descend the stairs.

"A couple of other things?" Scott asked as he chewed on the chicken leg.

"Okay, I told him you had been released, and if he didn't give me the information I wanted, you'd be there to have another go very shortly." Mary admitted defeat.

"Mmmm." Scott carried on chewing. "And what did he tell you?" He took another bite.

"He doesn't know who the buyer is, but he does know the courier who picked the merchandise up." Mary grabbed the keys and walked past him. She locked the back doors and walked to the front of the house again. "Ready?" she asked, unlocking the front door.

"Sure. Let's go beat some answers out of this courier," Scott said, throwing the chicken bone into the trash and wiping his hands on a towel before following Mary out the front door.

"Is that your plan?" Mary asked, locking the door behind them. "Beat everybody up until you find who you're looking for?"

"You catch on quick," Scott said, looking back at her with a smile.

"There are other ways to get people to talk, you know," Mary said, walking to the driver's side of the car.

"Oh, you're driving, are you?" Scott asked as he watched her open the door.

"Well, I've adjusted the seat. I'm just trying to save time." She smiled, knowing Scott wasn't buying her pitiful excuse. He got in and closed the door behind him. "It's about a two-and-a-half-hour drive. Which will give us plenty of time to talk on the way. There's something I want to know, and I hope you'll answer me truthfully." She started the car and pulled away from the curb.

Chapter 13

The Porsche cruised effortlessly along the freeway, passing everything on the road. Mary seemed confident driving at high speed in Porsche Cayenne turbo S beast. The throaty growl was enough to have most of the drivers in the road in front of them pull aside without much of an issue as they raced along the interstate.

"I've got something to ask you." Scott glanced at her. "The kid in the wheelchair, your brother, is he the name on the list? Is he in protective custody?" Scott asked, watching Mary's reactions closely.

"How did you know?" Mary asked with more than a hint of sadness in her voice.

"Every picture tells a story."

"And what story did my picture tell you?" Mary asked in a semi-defensive tone.

"I'm guessing your folks died not too long ago, and you had to give up competing in gymnastics with the new challenge of looking after your younger brother. Didn't have time to grieve properly because of all the new responsibilities. You struggled to keep things together, with a part-time care assistant to look after your brother, as you juggled that with your studies and working life." Scott watched her intensely as he talked. "Never had time to go on a proper date because of your hectic lifestyle, so you made bad choices in partners. And the partners you ended up with didn't stick around because they couldn't hack living with a gal who had the responsibility of a disabled brother living with her." Her eyes twitched as he spoke. "You studied hard to try and find a way to help your brother. Moved here to the US to get him better health care while you continued to study, and feel guilty that you're actually enjoying a little freedom doing what we're doing while your younger brother's held in protective custody."

Mary slowed the car and eased onto the shoulder. Her eyes filled with tears. Her bottom lip quivered as her posture dropped and her shoulders sunk.

"You're right. I'm a horrible person." She sobbed. "As much as I hate myself for it, I haven't been this free for years. I felt a burden lifted for a few days while somebody else was looking after him." She looked pitifully toward Scott. "It's not that I don't love him, I do. I just never get any time to myself, and I shouldn't feel guilty for being able to get out for a couple of days without having my entire life revolve around him. And I'm ashamed of myself for it." She shifted into park and wiped the tears from her eyes.

"Hey, I wasn't judging. It was just an observation. Of course, you deserve a little bit of time to yourself, everyone does. You shouldn't feel guilty about it. Why didn't you just get the care worker to do a few more hours now and again, so you get a bit of you time?"

"I can't afford it. Medical bills are racking up, my savings are running out. Everything my parents left me has gone, and balancing my studying with working and running the house is taking up more than I have already. I had to cut the hours of the care worker in the first place, just to be able to keep her on. I've made cut back after cut back, and I haven't got a clue what to do next." Mary paused for a moment as she dried her eyes and reflected on her thoughts for a second. "I'm sorry, I don't know why I'm telling you any of this." She hadn't opened up to anyone like this since she'd moved to the States. "So what about you?" Mary asked, wanting to shift the attention from herself. "Huh? Mr. I'm Gonna Rip Off Anybody's Head Who Doesn't Tell Me What I Want To Hear. What's got you so heavily invested into finding this maniac? Huh?" Mary looked at Scott, who was staring down into the foot well.

"Because I'm not too different from you."

"Ha! You're nothing like me, Sherlock Hogan! Look at a few pictures, and suddenly you think you know me, think you're like me. You're nothing like me. You're a violent thug who goes around beating people up to get answers, all for an FBI handler who uses you to do his dirty work and drops you like a piece of shit when he's finished with you. How are you anything like me?" Mary took off her seatbelt and sat staring at Scott for an answer.

"You weren't partnered with me by chance, Mary. You were selected. You were picked out for attributes you have and deliberately chosen. None of this was an accident. You're with me right now *because* I'm so much like you in so many ways. Because I feel the same guilt you're feeling now, every day of my life." Scott took a deep breath and exhaled.

"Go on," Mary said quietly, skeptically curious as to where this was going.

"Due to complications, my wife died in childbirth. My son suffered, too, he's got … issues." Scott couldn't bring himself to say the actual words and still had trouble admitting it to himself that his son was physically disabled. "I couldn't deal with it. I tried. I was lost without my wife. I spun out of control. Brandi, my son's godmother, took care of him most of the time."

"That's the girl at the house where your car was?" Mary interjected.

"Yeah, that's right. She's a bit rough around the edges, but my wife and Brandi were best friends, and she trusted her more than her own mother.

That's why she asked Brandi to be his godmother. She never had anything to give except love. Which is more than what I had. That's why I gave Brandi everything I'd got to look after my son. I couldn't do it. I was in no state to be a father to him. I was always promising myself I'd go back, and this time was going to be different. I'd be the dad he deserved. But then I'd go off the rails again and do something stupid. Every time I was alone, I'd look back and know it was subconscious self-sabotage. I'd hate myself for it. I'd promise that I'd stop fucking up and be man enough to be there for him, that I wouldn't do this shit again. And then, before I knew it, he's on the list of some psycho with just over a day to live. I've fucked up everything I've done since that kid was born. I'm not fucking this up, too!" Scott looked over at Mary, who had a look on her face revealing how she'd so seriously misjudged him.

"I …" Mary went to speak, but Scott interrupted her.

"Spare me the pity apology. Just drive, will ya? I want to stop this son of a bitch."

Mary's intuition told her it wasn't the time to continue so she dropped the conversation. She drove on without a word. It didn't take the Porsche long to get up to the speed of every other car on the freeway. Mary manoeuvred into the moving traffic and pulled out into the fast lane. She put her foot down, and the massive engine roared as they gained speed. She had decided to give Scott the chance to wind down and reflect on their conversation. For a fair amount of time, they both sat without a word.

Mary broke the silence first. "So, how long have you known Carver?"

"Too long," Scott replied with an exaggerated eyeroll.

"I take it you have quite a history together."

"Yep," Scott looked out of the side window for a moment, aware that she was trying to break the ice and ditch the atmosphere, but not sure where this was all heading.

"So, are you going to tell me about it?" Mary attempted to make it sound like her inquiry was light and just small talk.

"It's a long story," Scott said, not wanting to go into details.

"But is it a good story?" Mary asked with a smile, still trying to keep some form of conversation flowing, only the flow seemed more of a drip.

"Nope. Just long."

"I take it he knows you from when you were a spy?"

Scott wanted to correct her, but it wasn't worth the time or effort at the moment. He didn't like all the probing and wasn't sure what she was trying to attempt to extract from him or even if she was trying to extract anything at all. His past had caused his mind to grow naturally suspicious of anyone who asked too many questions. He decided a change in direction for this conversation was the best course of action.

"Something like that. What about you? How do you know him? Was he one of your bad choices on the men you dated since moving here?" Scott asked teasingly.

"No," Mary replied with a cheeky smile, knowing Scott's mood had now changed and he was teasing her. "Anyway, you make it sound like you think I've had loads of disastrous dates." Mary's mock defense caused Scott's smile to deepen.

"Are we nearly there yet?" Scott asked.

"What, me and you? What makes you think we were going anywhere?" Mary asked defensively.

"The courier's," Scott replied with a grin.

"Oh, of course. Yes, the courier's house. That's what you meant. I knew that." Mary straightened her shoulders and looked straight ahead with a serious look of concentration on her face.

"Sure you did," Scott said mockingly, a huge smirk on his face as he looked at Mary to see how she would respond.

"Asshole," she whispered with a grin, just loud enough for Scott to hear it.

"What?" Scott asked.

"What?" Mary replied, still smiling through pursed lips and a cheeky glint in her eyes.

"What did you say?"

"Nothing. I didn't say anything." The smile on Mary's face held as she kept her gaze fixed on the road, and Scott watched her, not knowing if he should continue or drop it while the going was good.

They pulled off the freeway and headed west through mist-shrouded rolling hills in the giant yawning valley. It wasn't long before they cruised into the start of civilization and more built-up areas. Passing luxury gated communities and small towns with every house painted the same color. All are run by homeowners associations that would guarantee a mild level of communism in the free world. The farther they drove, the more sparse the properties became. Eventually, they arrived at a mid-level and more densely populated area close to the edge of the downtown amenities. Mary checked the address she'd saved on her phone and was about to pull over.

"This is it," she said.

"Okay, keep driving past and go to the end to turn around," Scott instructed her.

"Why?"

"We get to have a look as we go past for the first time, then, on the way back, we pull up on the other side of the road. When we get out of the car, we can check the place out as we cross the road. Weigh things up a little."

Mary slowed down as they passed the house for the first time. Decorative painted bars on the windows, both upstairs and down, was the first thing to catch Scott's attention. A split-second thought had him asking if they were there to keep people out or to keep them in. His thoughts were overridden when a more urgent question posed itself. He spotted two sets of small CCTV cameras dotted around the outside. Not in different places but always in pairs. Mary swung the car around and drove back down, pulling up on the other side of the road.

"Well, this is our guy's place," Mary said. "Phil Draper. Courier for the rich and dodgy."

"Then let's go see what he can handle," Scott said, getting out of the car and taking his time to walk across the road. Observing as much as he could on the approach. "You always approach from the other side of the road. It gives you the maximum exposure time to the front of the house. That way, you're not walking past and rubber-necking as you turn to take in glances or trying to take in as much as you can when you're level with it. Crossing facing it lets you take in the whole picture in plenty of time to make as many observations as you can as you close in."

Mary listened carefully in fascination and watched closely as Scott walked over, scanning the area in detail, profiling the man who lived there before they'd even knock on the door.

Scott spotted a metallic blue Subaru with gold graphics on the drive. It looked the typical car of someone who had made the sound 'Barrp!' a few too many times and played way too much X-Box. A quick glimpse revealed no child seat in the back. The driver's seat wasn't upright or close to the steering wheel, so the chances were higher of the driver being male. His assumption was backed up by a singular magic tree. Experience told him that most female drivers tend to go overkill on the air fresheners at the very least and a few hairbands around the handbrake are common, too. He carried on scanning the car. Heavy tread wear on the outer rim of the front tires meant the driver had been cornering too fast, and the thin layer of black brake dust on the wheels meant he'd been braking late and heavy. It had all the signs of a typical boy racer, prat mobile.

The interior was the complete opposite of the reasonably clean exterior. The ashtray was full of broken cigarettes with unsmoked filter tips overflowing. Torn Rizzla packs dotted the entire car among dry tobacco, and ash peppered throughout. A few fast food joint souvenirs were abandoned with napkins tucked into different crevices, but the pièce de résistance was the massively expensive stereo, smack dab in the middle, which was probably worth more than the entire car, even if the fuel tank was full.

All of this helped Scott to build a profile of the vehicle's owner. It spoke volumes about his personality type. The car stood out, saying image meant a lot to this guy, but the messy interior with the odd stray couple of fries down the back of the seats implied just like the car, on the outside, things might look good, but on the inside, this guy's life was a bit of a mess.

Several levels of unhappiness, coated with a layer of lacking discipline, all topped with a pinch of inferiority complex to make a bitter prick pie.

The whole car screamed for attention. It was in complete contrast to the plain white Ford Econoline van parked on the other side of it. The inconspicuous panel van would blend in anywhere except for Scott's mind, where it may as well have had "Free Candy!" painted on the side.

"Hollywood gets a lot of things wrong but not that," Scott mumbled to himself, thinking of all the times the white panel van had been the weapon of choice for most kidnappers the world over.

They walked to the front door of the townhouse. Scott knocked. The door opened a crack, a safety chain holding it secure. The slight smell of weed and smoke drifted from the doorway before being taken by a slight breeze.

"Yeah?" The guy in a white vest top eyed them both suspiciously, his one hand held the back of the door, the other kept just out of sight behind the wall. Scott figured he was covering a handgun behind the wall, ready to point through the crack in the door in the event of trouble.

"I got a job I was told you could help me with," Scott said.

"I'm not doing any work at the moment," Draper replied.

"It's really urgent," Mary added.

"What is it?" the guy asked, looking between Mary and Scott.

"Can we talk inside?" Scott asked, making eye contact in a way that spelled his discomfort with talking on the street.

"Who sent you?" Draper asked.

"Big Al said you'd help us out," Mary said.

"Oh, then why didn't you just say so?" the guy said, unlocking the door and flashing a smile that showed a build-up of muck on his rotten teeth. His hand moved in to shove the pistol he was hiding back into his holster, just as Scott had suspected.

The smell of smoke got a little stronger with a hint of cheese in the mix.

The other side of the doorway, opposite where Draper stood, was a lounge room. A large and well-used sofa with the two-end seats worn more than the last dipped in testimony to hours of overuse. A coffee table housed control pads for the paused video game displayed on the huge television on the opposite side of the room and ashtrays with all the smoking paraphernalia any pothead could dream of. The only thing missing was Bob Marley playing in the background.

Empty takeout cartons littered the corner, and the almost threadbare carpet looked like the vacuum cleaner had never been invented. A modern glass stand held the massive new-looking television, with a modern games console tucked underneath. Other than that, the once white room was now more of a light nicotine yellow and pretty much empty. It was clear to see where Draper's priorities lay.

Scott stepped in politely, and as he got level to go past Draper, he grabbed Draper's throat with his left hand, simultaneously clutching at Draper's pistol with his right. He choked Draper as he hit him on the head with his own pistol. Draper's scrawny hands shot up to grab Scott's bulky forearms but couldn't budge them. A look of fear filled Draper's eyes as he realized Scott wasn't there in a friendly capacity. Mary slipped in behind them and gently clicked the front door shut.

"Is there anyone else in the house?" Scott growled, looking into Draper's eyes. Draper rapidly nodded with an accompanying gulp. Scott released his grip on Draper's throat slightly.

"My girlfriend. Upstairs." Draper pointed up with his eyes and strained to speak through Scott's slightly eased grip. Scott squeezed tightly again.

"Anyone else?" Scott asked, there was a pause for thought before Draper shook his head side to side in rapid succession. Scott held Draper firmly in place and looked over at Mary.

"Go take a look," Scott said, flicking his head and pointing up with his eyes. "Be careful." He added before turning his attention back to Draper. "You're about to have a really bad day." He growled.

A loud banging at Drapers front door startled Scott.

"You okay in there, Phil?" a voice shouted from outside the front door. "We saw some dude's Porsche out front. Need us to come in and take care of anything." Scott looked back at Draper, who now had a wide grin on his face.

"You're so fucked now," Draper said with a glint in his eye. "They're gonna rip you apart."

A bunch of crashing and banging sounds alerted Scott to a struggle upstairs. He looked into Draper's eyes again, who seemed to show no concern for the girlfriend he allegedly had up there. The door banged a couple of times again.

"Phil? We're coming in!" the voice from outside shouted, preceding the sound of a key going into the door lock.

Chapter 14

The downdraft from Napier's Jet-Ranger helicopter caused swirls of air to circulate on the deck of the *Naughty-Cull Dream* as Douglas gently touched down the skids onto the prestigious super yacht. Waves gently lapped against the side, with the slightest of sloshing noises being drowned out by the helicopter's engine. A smartly dressed young staff member ran out under the spinning rotor blades to open the helicopter door. Napier snapped his laptop shut and slid it into the custom-made leather case. The engine noise lowered, and the rotor blades slowed as the staff member opened the door. The scent of spent aviation fuel was accompanied by the heat from the engine. Napier removed the headset and hung it back up as he stepped from the helicopter, slipping the strap to his leather laptop case over his shoulder. The San Francisco coastline was barely visible from where Napier's yacht sat anchored on the Gulf of the Farallones.

The captivating scenery was wasted on him as he paced from the helicopter to the door being held open for him by another member of staff. He'd become so accustomed to the glorious views and the sheer beauty of the sun's reflective rays dancing on the ocean waves in splendor that he barely noticed the change in location. His focus was elsewhere, as only the change in noise, light, and ocean breeze, alerted his senses he'd stepped inside the exquisite interior of the flawless yacht.

Douglas had caught up and entered the room behind him as the staff member remained outside, clicking the door shut, which in some way seemed to seal the room from the din of mixed noises outside. The hidden technology of the vessel worked to act as a form of modern Faraday cage, keeping all possible means of communication within the room they were sitting in. Even the gap between the glass of the double-glazed windows was deliberately utilized with an invisible shield that buzzed around and disrupted the waves of any communication device which attempted to generate a signal in or out of the room.

Napier had not only invented and designed the equipment himself but was there to watch over the installation when the yacht's bespoke design was being put into production. He had field-tested it with next-gen technology in person and was satisfied that he could speak freely and openly within the confines of the comfortable saloon at the stern of his luxury yacht. Aside from the slight vibration from the engine room, the cavernous and salubrious surroundings were almost silent. A faint scent of cleanliness akin to that of freshly washed linen subtly filled the air, it's only competition was the fragrance of the sumptuous cream leather upholstery. Complimented by the deep pile cream carpet, the fine glossy dark wood furnishings were so highly polished that Douglas could see his reflection as he sat down facing Napier.

The two men had barely settled in their seats as the door opened, and a butler brought a cart of refreshments. An array of everything from chilled mineral water to a selection of fine finger foods were on offer, alongside a coffee pot and cream.

"Will there be anything else, sir?" the butler inquired.

"No, that will be everything, thank you." Napier spoke without expression as he dismissed the butler and focused on Douglas.

Douglas wasn't waiting for an invitation and sat keenly scooping spoonful's of brown raw sugar into a cup before filling it with hot coffee and sloshing the cream on the top.

Napier looked past his sins. He might be a little uncouth, but Douglas was loyal and backed up everything Napier had done. He had been there and proved he was prepared to give everything he had to Napier's quest without hesitation. Napier sometimes wished Douglas was a little more refined but looked past his flaws and chose not to see the lack of grace. Napier was fully aware it was an insufficiency in education, not a lack of dignity or desire to be civil. To anyone who didn't know better, they might think that Napier looked down on Douglas, viewing him as only a military man, a blunt instrument or a tool at Napier's disposal. This was far from the case. Napier saw Douglas as the second half of a partnership. The best jockey in the world cannot win a single race without a horse to do so. They both had different strengths and Napier was well aware of what each of their strengths were.

"What we're about to do will change the world forever, Douglas." Napier poured a glass of chilled mineral water. He set the half empty bottle next to the glass as beads of condensation tumbling down the side sparkled in the yacht's bright lights. He lifted it and took a sip, constantly maintaining eye contact with Douglas.

"Mmm." Douglas cut his swig of coffee short as he lowered the cup from his mouth to answer. "It most definitely will. It's been a long time coming but change is about to happen."

"There is something else I want to talk to you about, though. Changes might be made, that's for sure, but it will only be a matter of time before the world slips back into its old ways. Change is temporary. What we need is a reboot. There is too much global corruption and too many life sponges sucking away society without giving anything back, draining all they can from the world, with absolutely nothing to contribute. They're parasites and will never bring anything of substance or value to their respective communities. It's ironic how the opposite ends of the spectrum, both the scum and cream of society bring less, the further away from the center they're located. The very top and the very bottom, are the epitome of worthlessness. And as the population grows, the number of these parasites increase. Do you understand what I'm saying, Douglas?"

"Yes, I get it, a big chunk of monkeys need to go. I been hearing about all this kind of thing a lot recently. The world's over populated and all that stuff."

"On the contrary, Douglas. The over population of the world is a fallacy. If every single person in existence lived in an area as densely built as New York, they would all fit in an area the size of the state of Alaska. The whole world. All of them, in one state." Napier widened his eyes and watched carefully to see if Douglas was taking it in. "The problem is not the number of people, it's the number of leeches, taking from everywhere and giving nothing in return." Napier took another sip of his water and placed the glass back onto the table. "There are many good people who give so much to this world and have so much to offer, these are the type of people we need more of. These are the type of people we want to keep. When we have finished our work to change the system, we then need to change the people of system, too. You are the first person I've trusted with this concept but this is going to be the grand plan. Changing the rules was only the start. We need to deploy a method not too dissimilar to the one we've been using, to trim the dead wood from the top and bottom of society. The spoiled third generation rich kids who only know how to take and the members of congress who do nothing but feed themselves the money of corruption to support their lives gained through influence in politics alone. At the same time, we need to be rid of the scum who will never bring anything but misery to the world. The low lifes draining everything they can get to fuel their desire for self-satisfaction. From alcoholic, jobless, wife beaters, to drug addicts who steal and murder for their next fix, none of whom would ever have a fleeting thought of bettering themselves, never mind doing something selfless for the world or trying to give instead of take for a change. The ones that are beyond help and are simply a thorn in the side of the community in which they reside."

Douglas took another swig of his coffee and nodded. Napier ignored the fact that Douglas placed his cup directly on the polished wooden side table.

"So we're going to work on a depopulation theory? Like all the crazies talk about on YouTube?" Douglas had a look of excitement in his eyes, like a boy being told he was going to have birthday party.

"Something like that. Only we're going to be more targeted. It won't be a random round up of the masses to execute World War Two fashion. I've devised a system that will help determine who stays and who goes. It's all based on a very complex criteria selection software I've been working on.

It will look at everything from a person's genetics to their history and profile them accordingly. It will work out a trajectory of their life, determine if they're on an overall incline in their life or a one way path of self-destruction. It takes into account their last two generations to see if there's improvement." Napier paused for a second as Douglas lifted his cup, his eyes drawn to the beads of condensation forming a ring where the bottom of his cup sat moments ago. Douglas took a slurp and plonked it back on the table, lines of brown solidified coffee stained the sides of the cup where the hot liquid had ran down the outside from where Douglas had drank.

Napier ignored it and continued. "The point is, every aspect of a person's life will be taken into account. Whether they're going to cost or contribute to society. Whether it's in the form of innovation or art, poetry, music, science, whatever. If they have something of value to give they make the cut, even authors. If, however, they are nothing but wastrels, a tick in the form of a human, sucking the life and energy from this Earth, then then they will be selected to be removed from the planet." Napier sat back with an excited look in his eye, eager to know what Douglas thought of his plan.

"It sounds like you've given this a lot of thought. Are we talking about just America?"

"No, the whole world, the entire world needs to be included for this to work. You wouldn't prune only one area of a bush would you? No, in order for that bush to grow the way you want it to, you cut it back all over and shape areas to have it grow healthily in the shape and form you desire." Napier spoke proudly clasping his hands in front of him.

"I suppose," Douglas said thinking about Napier's explanation. "That's one hell of a lot of people gonna need your juice." Douglas realized the enormity of the task. The one he'd just done was a labor and that was only in one country.

"Don't worry. I've devised an ingenious delivery system, which will make our job so much easier." Napier beamed with pride.

"You could have told me that before you had me running around finding ways to inject ten thousand people with Nano fluid." Douglas had a tone of sarcasm in his voice but Napier ignored that, too.

"Let me show you," Napier said slapping his hands on his knees as he got up from his seat. His enthusiasm was contagious and Douglas immediately stood, swiping a handful of nibbles and stuffing them into his mouth as he walked behind him. Napier lead the way out of the room and down the stairs, heading below the deck of the enormous yacht.

Napier's smile filled his face as he spoke, his arm outstretched as he proudly boasted the magnificence of the delivery system.

"You see!" Napier was almost shouting with excitement. He looked back to see Douglas still standing at the bottom step. Almost like he was frozen in amazement. His mouth was slightly open while he took in the magnificence of Napier's mind, which had been constructed and stood in front of him. Napier went on to explain how the entire delivery scheme works, from the fluid being mass produced in the belly of the luxurious vessel, to the automated technology which was designed to deposit a lethal dose of his newest concentrated substance into the bloodstream of his filtered list of society members. The ones who passed through his system would be fine but the remnants from both ends of society would find themselves unwillingly getting administered with Napier's non-optional suicide solution.

"We can redefine the way the world operates. We can have a world where greedy men who are only out to make themselves richer don't exist and only the great and talented thrive in a society that wants the best for everyone, not just themselves." Napier had walked back over to where Douglas was standing. "And now I want to share the best the part with you. Come, follow me."

Douglas walked silently behind as Napier punched a code into a digital keypad. A slight hiss preceded a panel about a meter square opening from the wall and sliding to the side. Bright lights illuminated the insides of the compartment.

Napier could barely contain his excitement.

Douglas watched in amazement as Napier took the contents out, allowing him to bring his creation to life.

Chapter 15

Draper's front door swung open
to reveal three men armed with pistols,
the man at the front bigger than the
other two standing either side at his
rear. All of them looking like they had a
room temperature IQ at best. The big
one looked like he'd be more at home in
an amateur wrestling ring. The groupies
either side of him only had the balls to
be there because the presence of the
big guy. The big one was cocky
because of an equal mixture of his size
and overinflated ego due to his two
groupies. His false sense of self-power
was about to get a lesson in dysfunction
if he tried anything stupid.

"Put your gun's down or I'll shoot
him," Scott said sternly, as the three

men spotted Scott holding a pistol to Draper's head.

"Put your gun down or I'll shoot her!" A voice from behind Scott called.

Scott turned slowly to see Mary at the bottom of the stairs being held in a similar position to how he was holding Draper. The pistol pointed into Mary's right temple by Draper's girlfriend. Pretty but plain, she looked like she was once a beautiful girl. Now she looked like she'd been used and abused many times and submitted to a life which she'd come to accept. She pushed the pistol into Mary's temple and took another step forward.

"Now who's having a bad day?" Draper asked.

"You remember what I told you about 'Pardon me's' and 'Cheerio's'?"

Mary asked Scott with the slightest trace of a smile on her face.

"Now's your chance to shine," Scott replied.

Mary's hands shot upward and grabbed Draper's girlfriend's wrist with the speed and accuracy of a cobra snatching prey. She pulled the pistol forward so it no longer pointed at the side of her head. Mary leaned backward slightly, held all her weight on her left leg and from like what seemed out of nowhere, kicked her right leg up and over her own shoulder. Smacking Draper's girlfriend straight in the face. Scott's head was on a swivel back and forth between Mary and the thugs in the doorway. He spotted a flinching movement from the big guy for a moment and pointed his pistol forward with a warning look in his eye.

"Don't!" Is all Scott said before rapidly snatching the pistol back and pushing into the side of Draper's head again.

Draper's girlfriend froze in shock at how fast it all happened. Before she could regain her senses, Mary leaned forward still holding the girl's wrists tightly. Pulling the girl over Mary's shoulder and slamming her into the floor in front of her, Mary went a step further and cracked the pistol she'd now taken control of into the girl's nose. The girl yelled but Mary added another couple of slams to the head for good measure, knocking the girl out cold.

Keeping the pistol in her hand, she looked up at Scott who gave in impressed smile and turned his attention back to the three men in the doorway.

"Come on in, fellas," Scott said. "Let's have a chat, and drop the guns just there." Scott waved his pistol in a calling motion indicating to them to filter into the large room at the back of the house. The bigger guy's eyes shifted left and right for a second before resting back on Scott and the gun at Draper's head. He seemed to be weighing up his options but his thoughts all must have led to the same conclusion as his arms dropped by his side and his physiology changed to a state of submission as he tossed his pistol to the floor.

"Don't try anything stupid or I'll put more than thoughts into this guy's head." Scott grunted to reinforce the position they were in.

Mary collected the pistols they'd dropped near the front door and moved into the main room. She pulled four dining chairs from around a table, lining them up to face where Scott was standing. She quickly frisked the men in case they had any more guns or other hidden weapons.

Scott glanced around the main room. Bulk packs of sterile needles lay on a long table against the rear wall. Boxes of everything from crack pipes to bongs filled the other end. A second slightly higher table housed a spread of landline phones, each with a card taped to the wall behind it, with details and the number written on it in black ink. There was a pile of paperwork stacked to the side of every phone. A pen and pad accompanying each. Under the table was boxes of more dodgy looking junk. At the other end of the room behind the three new guests was a laptop on a desk, with a chest of drawers to the right. An abundance of new and used cell phones were on charge on the top of the drawers and a box under the desk with broken phones and sim cards filling it. A filing cabinet stood in the corner and the table from where the chairs were taken remained by the wall to the right. A Sports Illustrated calendar above it with scribbles on certain dates.

Scott stood in the doorway with the access to the kitchen and the stairs behind him.

"Sit down," Scott growled at Draper dragging him over to sit him on the fourth chair with his mates. As he plonked him in the seat he spotted a pack of cable ties on the top of the filing cabinet. He grabbed them and threw them over to Mary.

"Catch," he said as she neatly fielded them. She figured out he intended her to secure the men in the chairs and started wrapping them around their wrists behind each chair. As soon as she was done, she stood clear.

Scott looked down at Draper's girlfriend who wasn't showing any signs of coming around any time soon. He flashed a look and Mary came over and wrapped the girl's wrists, too, just to be on the safe side.

"There's another six girls upstairs," Mary said quietly to Scott.

"Doing what?" Scott asked in a tone of almost disbelief.

"Judging by the conditions, I should imagine they're getting ready to be sold to the highest bidder. It seems this place is quite the den of iniquity. The girls are all locked up and drugged. All of them a mess. The youngest is probably about eight or nine, none of them any older than seventeen."

Scott was beginning to boil.

Chapter 16

Douglas held the helicopter steady as they approached the coast heading back toward the castle. He hadn't said much on the flight to California. It was a lot to take in. He had looked up to Napier since he was released from prison and Napier took him under his wing. He'd given him a life he would never have come close to otherwise. The man was a genius, no two ways about it. Many levels above his own intelligence, there was no arguing that fact. But this was genocide. On a mass scale. Douglas piloted the helicopter seamlessly as his thoughts percolated.

He looked down as he flew over the land below. Thousands of tiny dots moving around like busy insects. Busy for who, though?

Maybe he's right, Douglas thought. *Maybe there are too many "no good" members of society. Maybe we need to cut the dead wood in order to run smoothly. It could make the world a better place. A new world of people working together.*

And Douglas would be a part of it. He would be in the history books as one of the founders of the new world. An architect of a population of great minds striving for only good. He liked that idea. Seeing himself as royalty like in status.

Before his imagination ran too far away with thoughts of grandeur, reality came back fast as the castle came into view. What he'd seen below the decks of the yacht had amazed him and yet terrified him at the same time. A genius system, so advanced, yet so simplistic in its theory gave one man the ability to wipe a complete demographic off the face of the Earth.

But what do I care? What have any of these fuckers ever done for me? Tours in the Middle East and treated like shit, given nothing for my sacrifices and sent to prison for my efforts when I get into shit when I had nowhere to turn. Fuck em! Napier's given everything to me and if he wants to take out a couple of billion losers around the world, then I'm with him!

Douglas had made his mind up. He was going to back up his boss no matter what.

Douglas twisted the cyclic back to lower the altitude of the helicopter and almost as though Napier had been waiting for him to finish his thoughts,

Napier's voice sounded through the headset.

"You've been more quiet than usual Douglas. I hope you're okay." His inquiring tone hinted at the slightest measure of concern.

"I'm still taking it all in. That was one hell of a reveal back there, boss. But don't worry about me. I'm behind you one hundred percent in everything you do." Douglas spoke with conviction as he circled the castle in preparation to land.

"Good to know, Douglas. Good to know."

The helicopter touched down on a raised area on one of the mid-levels of the castle roof and Douglas looked back to see the trace of a satisfied smile lingering on Napier's face. As the engines powered down, Douglas felt an enriched sensation of harmonious unity with Napier. A feeling of meaning and solidarity. Something he'd been missing for a long time. He was committed and was going to give his all to Napier no matter what.

Chapter 17

"Watch them," Scott commanded as he left Mary with her pistol aimed at the group of hostages tied to their chairs.

Ignoring the foul stench, he bounded up the stairs two at a time. The long landing was uncarpeted with bare dark wooden floorboards. The first bedroom on the left was obviously the master bedroom. A California king-sized bed was surrounded by laundry and litter with piles of clothes and bags and other junk narrowing in places, to leave a path to the en suite at the rear. The smell was rancid up here and Scott's nose twitched in disgust.

The first room on the right was also devoid of carpet with the windows blocked out and floor-to-ceiling bars like that of a jail house sat either side of a barred door. At one end a bucket sat in the corner with a putrid smell emanating from it. The walls were stained with fecal smears, blood, and grime.

Scott's eyes panned to the other end where two girls on thin foam camping mattresses lay completely naked and terrified, visibly shaking. Their hair was a greasy unwashed mess. Their bodies bruised and soiled. They were pale and visibly under-nourished. Too scared to speak or move. The conditions these girls were living in was repulsive and he felt a cocktail of emotions swirl inside him like a brewing storm, as anger, hate, sympathy, sadness and disgust churned through him. Scott wasn't sure exactly how old they were, he just estimated they were teenagers. He felt the need to retch as the smell in the room was physically sickening. The dire state of the place was horrific.

This side of the bars, a nightstand was littered with needles and a mixture of equally disturbing artefacts.

Scott held back tears for the girls. How could any human live with themselves while treating other humans like this? Scott had seen the despicably low levels people could sink to in his life but to treat children in the way these girls were being treated was beyond disgusting. He couldn't spend another second looking at the petrified girls shivering in their makeshift cage.

He left the room and turned to the next room. The second room was an exact replica of the first. Two more girls, only this time even younger. In Scott's estimation the first girl was no older than ten. Battered and bruised, her cut lips were healing and a black eye on the right side of her face was turning yellow round the purple circling. Bruises and marks covered the young girl's body and her matt blonde hair was tangled and messy. She was equally as petrified as the older girls if not more and didn't dare to even look up.

The second girl was maybe a little older, possibly about twelve. Track marks up her arms from the needles had her almost passed out on the floor and it was obvious from the state of her hands that she'd had all of her fingers broken at one point and they'd begun to heal but without the right medical attention leaving them mutilated.

He shook his head in disgust and walked to the last room. Anger was now coursing through his veins and bubbling in him. The pressure of rage building was only kept contained by the washes of sadness and sympathy that he felt for the children's suffering.

Just like the last room, two more girls in similar living conditions. A knocked over table with syringes scattered on the floor indicated this was where Mary had met Draper's girlfriend. Inside a cage, one girl was unconscious with a recent needle mark in her arm and a makeshift tourniquet dropped beside her. The other girl was more alert and not in as much of a dishevelled state as the others. Her long blonde hair was not as greasy and messy and she was not as emaciated as the first two girls. She still had some color in her skin and nowhere near as many bruises. She looked up at Scott with pity, her water filled blue eyes begging to know if he was there to help or hurt her.

"Help's on the way," Scott said in a low voice, almost croaking to force the words past the lump in his throat. He kneeled to look her in the eyes. "Someone will be coming to get you out of here but for now, I need you to just stay quiet and wait, okay? D'you understand?"

The girl's eyes lit up and she nodded before tears trickled down her face. Scott stood back up. He wanted to do more but that would have to wait. These girls were all going to need professional help. Counselling and proper care. Much more than he was capable of delivering. Scott was good at many things but he considered his paternal skills to be zero.

He left the room and moved back down the long corridor. A pang of guilt made his stomach twinge as his thoughts went back to his son. He could see his son. It was a choice. How many girls had been through here that would never see their families again? How many parents had that option been taken away from? The guilty feeling spread through his body as he thought of all the times he'd had the chance to see his son but talked himself out of it. Fear of messing up caused him to put it off once again. Maybe his subconscious logic was telling him that he couldn't mess up if he wasn't there.

He battled with his emotions as he walked the bare floorboards back to the top of the stairs. He questioned himself as he tried to settle his emotions. *I haven't got what it takes to*

be the kind of dad my son needs. I'm
not good with that kind of thing. What
kind of example would I set? Look at
me! It would only be a matter of time
before I let him down.

Scott reasoned with his logic, justified to himself as best he could why he hadn't been there for his son in the past. Seeing the girls he'd just walked away from though had him questioning everything. He might not be the best father but he'd make sure his son never went through anything like this. Maybe he wouldn't have been that much of a bad parent after all. Now, though, he could only hope and pray that he could stop the imminent attack or he'd never get the chance. A familiar feeling surfaced as he thought back to all the times that had passed that he could have spent with his son. His feelings of fear and guilt subsided as he neared the top of the stairs.

With each descending step he composed himself a little more and decided that anyone playing a part in this kind of torture was the lowest form of scum on the planet. It was time to get serious. With the last step he walked back into the rear room of the house and raised his gun.

"Okay, I'm going to ask some questions and I want you to tell me everything or shit gets nasty!" Scott shouted at the four guys strapped to their chairs.

"I aint telling you shit!" the big guy barked.

Without hesitation Scott took aim, then squeezed the trigger and shot the big guy in the forehead. Blood and brains splattered the wall behind him as the chair toppled backward and landed on the floor. The bang echoed throughout the room and a large dog out back barked a few times but it was muffled through the closed windows.

Everyone's ears rang for a few seconds after the shot went off. It was a risk but it sent a clear message. Despite the slight chance that the big guy could have been the only one with the information he needed, Scott had demonstrated his tolerance levels and shown he wasn't afraid to kill without warning. The color drained from the three remaining men, who sat stock still in a mixture of shock and fear.

"Well, he's no good to me alive if he ain't going to talk. So let's try you, Draper. Are you going to be a bit more talkative?"

"Okay. Sure. What do you want to know?" Draper spluttered in a state of panic, his right leg bouncing up and down rapidly and his hands visibly shaking through fear of not wanting to end up like his recently deceased friend.

"I want to know who these were sold to!" Scott said dangling the electronic device from Neil's house in front of him for all of the men to see.

"Delivered to, not sold to." Draper spat evidently panicked.

"What?" Scott frowned, not understanding the context of Draper's statement.

"They weren't sold. There was no profit chain in them things. We just got paid to deliver them."

"Shut up, Phil!" The guy on the far left grunted through gritted teeth.

Scott pointed the gun at the guy's head. "No! No! I'm sorry!"

Another bang filled the room and the second of the four men added to new décor on the rear wall. This time the chair didn't topple but what was left of his head slumped backward and dripped blood all over the floor. The dog out back barked again, this time for a little longer.

"Where?" Scott demanded turning his attention back to Phil.

"W … W … What?" Draper asked, feeling nauseated and scared after watching two of his friends slaughtered within a few minutes of each other.

"Where did you deliver them to?" Scott asked, louder this time.

"A castle! A fucking castle, man!" Draper shouted.

Scott raised the pistol.

Draper panicked. "No, I swear. It was a fucking castle! A fucking huge castle in Napa Valley. The address is on the pad there." Draper nodded toward the writing pad next to the laptop. Scott lowered his pistol and grabbed the notepad. He flicked a few pages back and there it was. The full address of the castle in Napa Valley.

"You better not be lying to me! Because if I have to come back here!" Scott growled.

"It's the truth. I swear!"

"Well, if it is, I got no reason to come back." Scott paused for a moment. "And no use for you anymore!" He raised the weapon and shot the last two men in the head. "Fucking scum!" He grunted under his breath. "None of these assholes deserve to take another breath."

"And what about this one?" Mary said, pointing down to Draper's girlfriend.

"Make sure she's tied up, then call the cops," Scott said still looking around the room.

"And she's not getting shot because …?"

"She's a victim," Scott said.

"What? And how exactly did you arrive at that conclusion?"

"Look at how she's dressed, like a kid almost. She would have been like one of the girls upstairs. Only dick splash over there took a liking to this one and decided to keep her. His boss would have turned a blind eye as long as he kept the supply of other girls coming." Scott went on to explain. "Look at the marks on her arms. He kept her an addict to ensure she complied and eventually Stockholm Syndrome would have kicked in. At some point he could let her off her leash and she would have willingly stayed. By now she would probably consider herself one of the lucky ones in comparison to what will happen to the other girls."

"Anything else getting you to this conclusion, Sherlock?"

"Yes, her hair color is natural. No dying or styling and unwashed. No makeup. All showing she knew no better. Finally, all the tattoos are home done, nothing professional. Implying she hasn't been out of this house for quite some time, all backed up by her pale skin tone. She doesn't get out much because it's too risky for our man over there. He entered this willingly. Him and his mates deserve nothing more than a bullet to the brain for their crimes, where as she deserves a second chance."

"That's quite a moral high ground you're standing on for someone who just shot and killed four men in cold blood." Mary looked at Scott for a reaction.

"Just one of my own personal quirks, I suppose." He tossed Draper's gun over the mess of blood and bodies.

"You're just going to leave the murder weapon here?" Mary said, concern showing on her face. "They'll find it. You'll go to prison."

"Ha. When this is all over I'm going back to prison anyway. You don't think they're going to let someone like me free to roam the streets, do you? I'm just their snarling dog they let off the chain to catch the bad guy. As soon as they're done with me, I'll be locked back in a hell hole to rot until they need me again."

Mary's face filled with a look of sadness, like she somehow knew he was right and what a sorry existence it was for him. Her thoughts of trying to imagine what it must be like to live his life were interrupted as Scott decided it was time to change the track.

"Give me a hand will you?" Scott walked to the kitchen. Judging by the contents of piles of black plastic bin liners, the girls upstairs were mainly living off fast food take-out whenever Draper could be bothered to do a food run. The refrigerator was home to an array of prepacked snacks but nothing substantial by any means. It didn't seem anyone here was a fan of cooking.

He opened a cupboard door to see nothing but pans and baking trays.

The next cupboard contained an open crate of water and some tins. He grabbed the plastic-wrapped water bottles and stood up.

"Grab whatever you can in the way of food for the girls upstairs."

He placed the pack of water by the bottom step and extracted a singular bottle. Mary opened a couple of drawers and found a roll of black bin liners. She started to grab what she could for the girls to eat and dropped it into the bag.

Walking over to the back door, Scott stepped outside anticipating the big dog would go for him. The desolate yard had a large pair of back gates secured from the inside with several tire tracks in the dusty makeshift driveway. The barren area to the right was dotted with baked dog mess that had been left to decompose. The smell was vile. To the right, cornered between the house and the side fence, a large cage with two battered steel bowls sitting beside it had a sorry-looking large black and tan dog laying there, chained to it.

With no regard for self-preservation, Scott walked toward the dog and the big old soft scrammel stood up and wagged his tail. Scott petted him and ruffled his ears as the dog let out a playful and friendly whimper. Both of his bowls were empty. The one with rotten brown food stains indicated the other dry one with the white residue was the dog's water bowl. Scott opened the bottle of cool water and filled the bowl. The dog instantly lapped away at it. Scott stroked the dog's back and with a couple of pats stood back up and walked inside again.

Mary had taken the water and food up to the girls and was descending the stairs. Scott stood at the foot of the stairway and looked up at Mary.

"Call it in. Get Carver to get help here as quickly as possible. We'll wait just out of sight until help pulls up, then we go before questions start getting asked."

Scott watched as Mary dialed Carver on her cell phone, then he grabbed a can of soda from the fridge and cracked it open.

"You want one?" he asked as Mary raised the phone to her ear.

She shook her head and Scott moved toward the front door. Mary walked out bringing Carver up to date with the details of events so far. Scott pulled the door almost closed and they both sat back in the car. Immediate appreciation for the scent of the car's leather interior and the less offensive smell of the magic tree made Scott feel more at ease after the event's he'd just witnessed. He was relieved to be out of there. And if that's what he felt, he could only imagine how it would feel for those girls when they got out and were taken to safety. Within minutes Scott spotted three squad cars and an unmarked come wailing down the street.

"Come on, let's get out of here."

Scott started the engine. They pulled away moments before the police cars screeched to a halt outside Draper's house. The Porsche rumbled along the road and they headed back toward the freeway.

His mind moved on to the next challenge. "Right, let's go and invade a castle," Scott said, overflowing with enthusiasm.

"There's something I never thought I'd hear someone say to me in my lifetime." Mary smiled.

Chapter 18

Raymond Napier clicked away at his computer station until he was distracted by the vibration of a cell phone in his pocket. He pulled it out with haste and for good reason. This wasn't his regular phone. This was an especially assigned phone and only one person had the number.

He answered and stepped away from his computers. He turned to his left to admire an enormous oil painting of a galleon in all its glory, listing in full sail through a treacherous storm, amid murky ocean waters. The call was brief and to the point. Napier didn't say much, he just took the information on board and ended the call.

Lina sat on a cream chaise longue with gold pattern behind him,

Douglas Wilde at a table to her left, midway through stripping and oiling his pistol.

"The FBI have dispatched a man called Scott Lomax to come after me. Have you heard of him?" Napier asked Douglas.

"No," Douglas replied, trying to recall if he'd heard the name anywhere before.

"Is he going to be a problem?"

"One man?" Douglas laughed as he answered and carried on cleaning his pistol. "No, no problem."

"Good then we proceed as planned." Napier responded satisfied in the abilities of his right hand man.

* * *

Scott and Mary drove North West toward Napa Valley. It was a fair distance so Mary give it some gas along the freeway. She glanced over at Scott a couple of times with a slight smirk she wasn't trying too hard to hide.

"What?" he asked.

"Nothing." Mary looked back at the road, then glanced at Scott again with a smile followed by her eyes returning to the road once more.

"What?" he insisted.

"Anyone who doesn't know you would get you all wrong. They'd look at you and see a brute, an ogre."

"Thanks," Scott replied sarcastically.

"No, I mean, people would look at you as the big violent guy. View you like some knuckle dragging muscle head with a bad temper but you're not like that at all." Mary glanced over at Scott again before continuing. "You have a human side. A deep protective side. And your own sense of right and wrong, be it a very screwed up version of a moral compass."

"Well gee, Doc, I'm feeling better already."

"No, I don't mean it like it's coming out." Mary grinned. "There's actually a caring loving guy under that scary mask. You're not the monster everyone sees. You're not some mindless violent thug. You're much smarter than people give you credit for. I mean, you had me worked out like that."

"Not completely, just a conclusion from what I could see."

"You see, what kind of a person makes these kind of deductions from their observations of pictures at a person's house?"

"Serial killers usually," Scott replied.

"Or detectives. See this is a perfect example of your thoughts. I think you put yourself in that box sometimes, because you *like* to be thought of as the bad guy. It makes it easier for you. But you're not a monster. You're an intelligent, deep, and good man."

"I'll let you know if I ever need a character reference." Scott grunted.

"Urrgh, and very frustrating!" she snapped back half in jest.

"So tell me, did you manage to find anything close to a Mr. Poppins since you've been in the States?" Scott asked wanting to change the subject and get the focus away from his flaws.

"I'm more of a chimney sweep guy myself, but no. I haven't come across anyone good enough to satisfy me with their chimney brush yet."

"I prefer to pay extra attention to the fireplace myself, way before I thrust my brush up there," Scott replied with a cheeky grin.

"Careful Mr. Lomax, talking like that, you could end up with soot on your bed sheets." Mary grinned as she kept her eyes on the road ahead. A ping sounded and the fuel light lit up on the dashboard.

"I better pull in at the next service station for petrol," Mary said.

"Petrol?" Scott said mockingly. "We might need some gas, too."

"Why do you guys call it gas when it's clearly a liquid?"

"It originally come from the word Cazeline after John Cassell, founder of the publisher Cassell & Co. who were the first to sell it commercially." Scott stated in a very matter-of-fact tone.

"Well you learn something new every day, don't you," Mary replied rhetorically but Scott wasn't listening. He scanned the area as she pulled up the slip road and turned right into the service station.

"Pull over there to the right," he instructed pointing to any area to the side of the gas station lined with parking bays.

Mary wasn't sure why they were parking and not pulling up to a pump but she followed Scott's instructions and drove nose first into a parking bay.

Scott looked over to the car next to them. A modern SUV as clean as the day it came out of the showroom. Probably never been over forty mph and cherished by an old couple. There was a few empty parking spaces and then a station minivan. It had seen better days. More than likely a family owned car where priorities of taking care of the car had slipped down the list. Eight seater means a struggle with probably more than three kids.

Two spaces up was an immaculately clean Honda. All the gloss and none of the dosh. A top aviator watch and an expensive tie complementing a cheap suit. Everything paid for on credit card.

In the last space was a Mitsubishi. Blacked out windows and looking like it needed a chimney pipe of its own with all the smoke flowing from the crack at the top of the driver's window. *Perfect.*

Scott clambered out of the Porsche and slowly walked over to the car. The smell of weed overpowered the scent of gasoline vapors that had previously filled the air. He casually stood on the grass at the side of the service station. Turning to face out he made a movement with his arms as if he was trying to light a cigarette. Giving it a minute and shaking his left arm as if his lighter was low on gas, he pretended to try again. He made it appear like he'd put it back in his pocket and gave a convincing impression he was looking around for someone else who smoked.

Looking like the Mitsubishi had caught his eye, he casually walked over and tapped the window gently. The electric window slid down, and a cloud of smoke escaped from the interior.

"Hey, man. You got a light?" Scott asked the guy in the car as he looked inside. Just the driver and his girlfriend in the passenger seat. Nobody in the back. Squares ripped from the corners of cigarette paper packets, and loose tobacco spilled over the center console. Cords to charge cell phones slotted into the car's lighter socket, and an array of magic trees doing little to nothing to hide the smell of weed all decorated the interior of the car.

"Yeah, man, here," the car owner said, digging into a leather man bag on his lap. As he looked up, shock filled his face to see Scott resting a pistol on the door of the car aimed at the driver.

"I just want money," Scott said. "Don't make a drama out of this. Hand me over some cash."

The owner of the car dropped the lighter and dug around in his man bag again. He pulled out four crumpled twenty-dollar bills. The girl was going through her purse, too, frantically rummaging around to see what she had.

"That's enough," Scott said, but the driver was still rooting for cash in his bag. The girl stretched her arm out with a fist full of more than twenty dollar bills. "That's all I need." He backed up a little. "Don't do anything stupid, give it about ten minutes after I drive away and call the cops. Tell 'em I pulled a gun on you."

Scott told Mary to pull the car onto a pump and slowly wandered into the service station. He was hoping to get the gas, pay, and be out of there before it got noisy. He had to put faith in the fact that the people he'd just stolen the money from would do what he instructed and not create a drama straight away. They could be on the phone with the cops now, as far as he knew, so he had to get things done as quickly as possible and get going.

Scott placed sixty dollars on the counter and slid it toward the cashier. "Pump seventeen," he said and turned to walk out.

They filled the tank leaving a happy cashier to keep the change, and jumped back on the interstate.

"You don't seem too phased by violence and murders," Scott said to get a conversation started.

"I told you, I'm no stranger to it. I dated a London gangster for two years while I was at college. They're a nasty lot. So, believe me, I've seen some gruesome events." Mary spoke with equal elements of shame and pride. It would have been difficult for most people to detect, but Scott was no stranger to spotting it.

When they finally got there, giant imposing walls hugged the castle grounds, giving way only to a gatehouse that housed heavily armed security guards who manned the wrought iron gates. The one casually smoking out front had as Italian mercenary look. Oversized biceps and matching oversized belly. His ball cap covered what Scott expected to be a receding hairline with too much gel. As large as the guard was, his overall shape spelled sedentary more than sentry.

Scott estimated four to six guards total, and if all of them were in the same physical shape as Don Ravioli, then they might be easy to pounce on, but they'll all more than likely start shooting in every direction before their brain has even registered what's going on. Butts and bullets everywhere were not what they really needed. A mid-day firefight could get messy. Five to six accurately placed bullets to assassinate with speed and skill was what Scott wanted. Figuring out how to sneak up on the Cornetto Corp was going to be another story. Each of them would be twitching with their hands over their pistols the minute a big guy like Scott marched up, and it could get noisy fast.

"Well, this looks fun," Scott said, looking at the huge guards standing at the gate. "Judging by the DWS badges embroidered onto their sleeves, I'm guessing these guys work for our Vicap star."

"What's Vicap?" Mary asked.

"The FBI's Violent Criminal Apprehension System. My best guess is these guys are a bunch of his ex-military mates. Probably all dishonorably discharged and can't get work anywhere else but for a criminal thug who has no issues with giving them all a gun and a job as long as they do as their told. Dangerous and dodgy, with more bullets than brain cells." Scott took a deep breath. "I'm going to have to think of a way to get past those guys first."

"I've got an idea," Mary said, turning the car around and driving back toward a dollar store she'd spotted on the way there. It hadn't taken her long to run and buy a pair of scissors before coming back out to the car. She clambered into the back and lay across the seat.

"Get out of the car for a minute," she told Scott, who was still sitting in the front.

"You're kicking me out of my own car. First, you take over driving, and now you're kicking me out of my car?" Scott rolled his eyes and reached for the door handle.

"It's just for a minute," Mary said.

Scott complied and stood out in the parking lot, leaving her to do whatever she was up to inside. A few minutes later she emerged from the back of the car. She'd cut her jeans into a tiny pair of denim hot pants.

"What do you think?" she asked, raising her arms above her head before spinning to face away. She'd cut the back high to reveal the bottoms of the cheeks of her butt, not leaving much to the imagination. To most people, it may have come across as playful, but she knew exactly what she was doing. Her arms were still in the air, and she gave a little wiggle.

"Wit-woooh. You want some fries with that shake?" Scott chuckled. "I'm not sure what your plan is, but I'm enjoying it so far."

Once back inside the Porsche, they rolled to a stop outside the security gatehouse. Mary stepped out of the car and, with a wiggle, a jiggle, and a giggle, bounced up to the guard standing out front.

"Hi, can you help me, please? My car's making a funny noise. I think it might need lubricant, but I'm not sure where to rub it," Mary said to the guard, who looked like all his Christmases had come at once. She bent over the hood of the Porsche. "I don't know how you open these things."

"Don't worry, I'll help you." The guard walked out to the car and gave his colleagues a wink through the window as he strutted over. His workmates smiled, rolled their eyes, or shook their heads.

Mary wandered to the back of the car and opened the trunk. "Oh, I think I've found something. Can you come here, and I'll give it to you?"

The guard wandered around the back of the car with a smile that instantly dropped as soon as he saw Scott push a pistol to his head when he stepped under the door of the open trunk.

"Get in!" Scott snarled, his nose wrinkled.

The frightened guard followed Scott's order, his eyes expanding with fear. Before he had chance to think about it, he was clambering into the huge trunk of the Porsche. Scott bashed him hard with the butt of the pistol and knocked him unconscious. Pulling the trunk lid down, the car rocked around outside the gatehouse.

* * *

"Lucky son of a bitch," the guard's workmates said as they watched on the screen through the CCTV. They didn't pay too much attention after that when the guard got out of the trunk and slowly wandered back to his post. The CCTV wasn't the clearest in the world, but they didn't think too much of it. Until their colleague swiped his pass to wander into the gatehouse and held his pistol out. Rapid, controlled shots, two at a time, dropped every guard in the room before any of them had time to think. The guardhouse smelled more like a teenage boy's bedroom than a security office. Scott pulled his newly acquired security hat off and flung it to the other side of the room. He'd caught them all off guard and was happy it had worked without too much drama.

Scott cleared the rest of the guardhouse, checking the changing rooms and toilet to make sure he hadn't missed anyone. A small kitchen area at the back had a sink and cupboards with a microwave on the side and a coffee machine next to it with half a jug of filtered coffee sitting on the hotplate. He opened the refrigerator, and saw a ham and salad bread bun packed in clear wrap with a sticker with the name Scott on it.

"Hmmm, they left me a sandwich," Scott mumbled to himself as he unwrapped it and poured himself a coffee from the machine at the back of the kitchen area. He walked back through to the main office and took a look around to see if there was anything that could prove useful. He finished the sandwich and slurped the last of the coffee as he paced the room, weaving in and out of bodies and making observations.

Mary left the near-naked security guard, tied up in the back of the Porsche, and trotted in to see Scott studying a wall-mounted map of the grounds.

"Let's go and get this son of a bitch!" Scott said.

"Wait. There's something I need you to know before we go in." Mary stared Scott directly in the eyes.

Chapter 19

Scott decided to leave his car where it was and try to sneak up to the castle entrance. Roaring up in a Porsche wasn't exactly tactical. He may as well phone up and tell them he's outside. Luckily there was enough distance between the castle and the gatehouse for the drama that had unfolded a few minutes ago to remain unnoticed. Normally it wouldn't have bothered him to pull up with a ballsy approach, but he didn't know how many people were inside, and he wanted to get to Napier without alerting him first, so the more subtle approach won the toss.

Mary and Scott tried to remain in cover as they made their way through the castle grounds.

"So, what did you want to know?" Scott asked as they tramped through the inner gardens toward the main area of the castle.

"If we get through this, I want you to make me a promise," Mary said as she tried her hardest not to sink into the dirt with the heels of her knee-high boots.

"Okay?" Scott replied dubiously.

"I want you to spend an hour with your son. Just an hour, get to know him. Don't worry about what comes afterward. Just promise me you'll do that one thing for me. For him. For you."

"Okay, just as long as you promise to help me out with something, too."

"What?"

"Conjugal visits." Scott laughed.

Mary gave him a playful slap to the upper arm, and they continued through the gardens.

They stayed as hidden as possible as they neared the castle's main entrance. The huge black wooden doors were open, but the giant heavy steel portcullis gate was lowered to the floor. The turnstile and chains to raise the gate on the other side were more for show. They weren't turned manually. A hidden electric motor turned them instead of man power. It was controlled by a switch panel somewhere on the other side of the courtyard.

"There's no way I can get through this. And I can't lift it." Scott looked around for other possible ways inside.

"You can't get in here, but I can."

"How?"

"Watch." Using the portcullis as a sort of ladder to ascend, Mary climbed to the very top and squeezed the top of her tiny framed torso through the slight gap. Her slender frame slipped through and she bent over so she was upside down the other side of the top of the gate. Without the slightest fear of getting stuck, she did the splits in mid-air and with controlled ease, lowered her legs down in front of her. Facing out and hanging by her arms alone, she managed to rotate and get a footing on the portcullis. She switched her arms back to where they should be and lowered herself down like she was coming down a ladder.

"I was thinking about doing that," Scott said with a smile.

"Carry on then. I'll wait." Mary teased.

"Ah, you're inside now. Press the button."

Mary crossed the courtyard and clicked the button to raise the gate. The electric motor whirred slowly and quietly, and the well-lubricated gate slid up its tracks steadily. As soon as it was high enough, Scott rolled under Indiana Jones style, and Mary clicked the other button to lower it again. They paired up again and walked across the courtyard together.

"You're still in pretty good shape, ain't you?" Scott said with a tone of admiration.

"Yes, I have a Peloton."

"I bet you do! Does it take batteries?" Scott asked in jest.

"No, silly, It's an exercise machine," Mary said, slapping Scott's arm with a slightly salacious smile as they walked across the graveled yard. The door in the far right corner of the courtyard was unlocked, and Scott slipped in with Mary following closely behind.

A dimly lit corridor led into the main body of the castle. It was warmer than Scott expected, with a scent of rose potpourri in the air. Carved stone insets in the walls allowed for decorative ornaments of war, like polished helmets, to be displayed. Scott drew his pistol and controlled his breathing. He stepped forward, remaining silent—slow, controlled steps.

He couldn't mess this up now. There was so much to lose. Scott would never have the chance to put things right with his son. The need to overcome his fears and put things right was a psychological challenge that he would have to struggle with. He had his doubts that he might never be able to face this fear but it was his quest, his challenge, his choice. And nobody should be in a position to take that choice away from him. His son had suffered enough, and Scott knew it was beyond any kind of fairness that he should suffer any more.

Nobody should suffer. Not only his own son but Mary's brother would suffer. Mary would suffer. She'd never forgive herself if they failed. Ten thousand Americans would die. If he lived himself, he'd spend the rest of his days hated in some dark, dingy prison cell. And to make things worse, nobody would be able to stop this maniac from striking again, so there was no way he could fail now.

He edged closer to a huge purple velvet curtain and moved to cover himself behind it. He steadied his breathing and reminded himself what was at stake. *Just sneak in stealthily*, he thought as he pushed closer to the curtain.

His hips brushed against an object on the other side, not realizing he'd sent a huge suit of armor falling forward. He looked around the curtain just in time to see it toppling forward, then ducked his head and squinted as he cringed. Frozen, he watched as it fell like a giant tree toward the floor. It seemed to be happening in slow motion.

Panic filled him, and his heartrate soared. His pulse quickened, and every hair on his body stood on end. The suit of armor, accompanied by a huge, heavy battle ax, went crashing into the concrete floor, sounding like a brass band having a sneezing fit, as it clattered into the solid bare stone.

"Agh, bollucks!" Scott shouted. "Hey, if you're here, I'm coming to fucking kill you!" He figured the element of surprise was now somewhere close to his virginity. Long gone, never to be retrieved.

He stepped out and ran across the large open hallway, gun drawn. No sign of life or movement. Mary scurried across behind him.

"Okay," Scott said. "We go up the stairs, you go left, I go right. It all meets up so we can cover ground faster. Don't take any unnecessary chances, and I'll hopefully meet you somewhere in the middle."

Mary nodded, then bounded up the huge spiral, stone stairway.

He got to the top faster and turned left. Mary was a couple of steps behind him and stopped as she got to the top step. She dropped her arms by her sides.

"I was meant to go left!" she whispered under her breath with a hint of agitation but Scott was too far ahead to hear her. She gritted her teeth and let out a sigh, then walked around to her right. A few steps in and she could hear the sound of muffled voices. She moved closer and kept in tight to the wall. The long landing opened up into a cavernous ball room style hall. A painting of a ship filled the wall to her right. Filled with sumptuous refineries fit for royalty to live. Rich purple velvet drapes and red carpets, complemented cream upholstery with gold pattern. To the left of the room, a vast open fireplace with a marble surround stood proud as a home to the enormous gilt gold framed, bevel-edged mirror above it. Farther along, an arch-shaped exit door sat between matching sconces on either side. The wall angled instead of a ninety-degree corner, a towering grandfather clock sitting pride of place, slowly ticked away. Three large crystal chandeliers hung from brass chains attached to the high ceiling above.

Glossy Italian furniture and elaborate silverware spread evenly around a contrasting center piece, sprawling with modern technology and paperwork. All of it laid a foundation for a bank of screens. Three smaller ones at the bottom and a large one hovering above all three. The large one seemed to display a satellite network around the globe. The smaller ones were lit up with data codes scrolling on the right, split screen CCTV footage from about twenty cameras on the left. The view of the middle one was blocked by a man in a black suit.

Mary looked to the right and saw a huge, scary-looking man with a baseball bat held ready to swing. Just to the side of him, Scott was peering around the corner of an opening at the top of another smaller and tighter spiral stairwell. If Scott stepped out, the viscous, ugly-looking guy with the bat would swing at him. It probably wasn't the best thing to do, but she decided she needed to create a distraction. She saw a jardinière holding a large plant and decided to take a run at it. If she smashed it, it would grab the creep's attention long enough for Scott to get the upper hand.

She lunged forward, but her attempt was thwarted as Lina then dived into her and started to lash out. Scott moved forward, focused on Mary, and failed to see Douglas Wilde swing a bat right into him, sending him flying backward and tumbling down the stairwell.

Raymond Napier punched a few more keys on the computer, grabbed his laptop and slid it into a travel bag, then casually strolled to the arched exit door at the far side of the room. Scott was nowhere to be seen.

Lina managed to flip herself on top of Mary and using her full body weight, push down on her hands that were now wrapped around Mary's neck. Mary thrashed as Lina choked her. She looked again at the stairwell as she struggled, but still no sign of Scott.

Chapter 20

Scott scrambled to get back up the spiral staircase as quickly as he could. By the time he'd reached the top he was boiling with rage, ready to rip apart the guy who'd slammed a bat into him and sent him tumbling down the stairs. As he ascended to the top step he immediately looked left and right to check for anybody waiting to swing at him. He wasn't falling for that again. Once he knew it was clear, he looked forward and saw Douglas approaching the arch door. Scott sprinted at him but stopped when Douglas pulled out a handgun and aimed at Scott's center mass.

"What you gonna do, Lomax? You ain't bulletproof!" Douglas said.

Scott was thrown temporarily, trying to figure out how this guy knew his name. *How did he know me? How did he know I was coming?* He watched as Douglas backed out of the door and closed it behind him. He heard the sound of a bolt sliding across and locking the door tight. Scott ran forward and kicked the door. The thick solid oak door didn't budge. Even if it opened in the direction Scott was kicking, the dense wood and wrought iron hinges held it as secure as could be.

Scott was still fuming. He looked around to see Lina on top of Mary, choking the life out of her, Mary turning different colors by the second.

"Mary!" Scott shouted as he ran over and grabbed Lina by the hair. He yanked her backward off Mary, dragging her away. Lina was kicking and screaming at first, but she soon realized she wasn't going to win this one, and her anger dissolved into submission.

Mary got up, coughing and spluttering, bent over at the waist like she was going to be sick. The coughs slowed as she seemed to be catching her breath.

"You all right?" Scott asked, still holding Lina by the hair. Mary just held a hand, fully extending her arm for a moment as she finished the last of her coughing fit. She stood up straight and walked over to Lina, where she slapped Lina across the face with a clap sound that echoed throughout the castle.

"That's for trying to choke me!" she yelled, not stopping as she slapped Scott in just the same way. "And that's for taking your time!"

"Ouch," Scott said, rubbing the side of his face.

"What the hell happened to you?" Mary asked.

"I was waiting at the top of the stairs, and I looked up and saw you lurking in the shadows, with Morticia Addams here, waiting to jump on you as soon as you popped out. I jumped up to run over to help you, and the next thing I knew, I was bollucks over brains and falling backward down the stairs. When I came back up, she was choking you, and Shrek was locking the door behind him." Scott turned his attention to Lina. "Where does that door lead?"

"To ze roof," Lina replied.

"Is there another way out?"

"Ze door at ze back, to ze left of ze stair-vell. Turn left and left again, zen it meets at a right turn where both corridors go to ze same place." Lina looked away.

"You got this?" Scott asked, referring to Mary's abilities to handle Lina.

"Oh yes, don't worry, she won't get the better of me twice. Go!" Mary replied.

Scott turned to pursue the two men they'd come here for. He followed Lina's direction, and as she said, Scott was led to a stairwell. The thundering roar of a helicopter engine could be heard at the bottom of the stairway. Unlike a car, you can't just start a helicopter's engine and fly away. Aside from getting the rotor speed up, the engine temperature had to be right, and the gearbox and engine were running in unison. It takes time, so you can't take off before the helicopter's ready. The closer he got to the top of the stairway, the louder the chopper sounded. The downdraft battered the castle roof as they were almost ready to ascend.

Scott did a scan left and right before edging out of the doorway. The helicopter was so noisy he hardly heard the bang from Douglas's pistol. Douglas fired another couple of shots off from the cockpit but was too busy trying to take care of the controls to aim properly through the tiny opening of the helicopter's window.

Scott slipped back inside to avoid the bullets that were ricocheting off the stone castle walls around him. He looked out to see the helicopter slowly begin to rise. It lifted a little as it went into a hover for a couple of seconds, then Douglas gave it some throttle, and the chopper rose a lot faster. Scott spotted Napier open his laptop pecking away at the keys. There was no point in waiting around to see the helicopter disappear into the clouds, so he ran back down to Mary.

"They got away," Scott said, exacerbated. "They had a chopper on the roof." Scott looked over to see Lina trying her hardest to conceal a satisfied smile. "Where are they going?" Scott roared at Lina.

"You vill never get to zem," she replied.

"Where?" Scott boomed, making both Lina and Mary jump.

"Mexico. He's got a compound in Mexico. Ze details are all over zere, amongst ze paper-vork, on ze desk."

Mary moved over to the desk, searching through all the files by the computer terminals below the bank of screens.

"I think I've got it," Mary said, pulling out a particular folder and walking over to show Lina. "This one?" she asked, but Lina started to shake. Shakes that became more violent. Lina's eyes rolled, and the convulsions started. Her body went rigid, she fell flat on the floor, and spasms ran through her body before she finally dropped limp.

Lina was gone.

"I don't get it," Scott said, his forehead wrinkled. "If he can kill anyone, why didn't he just kill us?" he asked as Mary flicked through the other files and clicked away on the computers.

"Because he can't!" she said with a huge grin at making her new discovery from all the work Napier had left behind.

Scott moved in closer as Mary explained.

"So you see it works something like this. Napier has to get each subject to somehow ingest a nanotechnology chemical. It can be delivered as a gas or liquid, breathed in, drank, eaten, or injected. But if you haven't had the nano liquid first, his system won't work." Mary told him as she looked deeper into his work and through his papers.

"So basically, he poisons his victims?" Scott asked.

"Kind of, he has to get the liquid into the body before he can activate it using radio waves," Mary explained.

"And how does he do that?"

"Looking at his early research, it looks like he took over an old, obsolete government spy satellite network called

Aquacade and tried to use microwaves,"
Mary said.

"And how did he manage to get
access to all that?" Scott asked.

"I'm not sure, but it seems it didn't
work because he then went on to write a
software program that hijacks cell
towers. So basically, he converted the
signaling system to be able to emit
sound waves that he could control. If
you've been subjected to the nano liquid
and are in an area with a cell phone
signal, he can adjust the spectrum of
soundwaves accordingly, and bam! He
kills you remotely."

"Using the system to activate the
poison?" Scott asked.

"The soundwaves would have
difficulty isolating the red blood cells.
You see, a red blood cell can do a
complete circuit around the entire body

in twenty seconds. The nano fluid latches on to the blood cell and, for want of a better description, fractures it. It then temporarily leaves a trace element behind, as it moves to the next cell. That trace element highlights the red blood cell to the incoming soundwave, allowing the cell to sort of 'stand out' and be targeted specifically by the incoming soundwave attack without affecting anyone else around them. It's a complicated system, but he's somehow managed to create the fluid in a way that will make it remain dormant in the body unless it's activated." Mary looked up, the fascination of the discovery had captivated her, but her focus shifted, and a visible display of urgency flashed across her face as she realized the clock was ticking.

They didn't have long before Napier activated his poison.

"We better get a move on," Scott said his sense of urgency growing. "Call Carver and tell him what we found. Then we better go find this place in Mexico."

Scott watched Mary take her phone from her purse to make the call. Scott was about to leave when something caught his eye. He spotted a folder that for some reason looked out of place. He opened it and discovered something that shook him to the very core.

Chapter 21

Mary had followed Carver's instructions over the phone from Napier's computer set up to allow remote access from the FBI field office. That way, he could access all of Napier's files and save time, so Mary didn't have to explain. She gave him the rest of the information as Scott dragged the near-naked security guard from the back of the car to lock him in the gatehouse.

"Tell Carver I said thanks for springing me from jail," Scott said while Mary was still on the phone. He closed the trunk and jumped in the passenger seat. Mary ended the call and started the car.

"Carver's reviewing the files now with his team. He said we did well to find this guy. Also, he's going to try and work on providing any assistance he can from his end, and he said he didn't get you out of jail."

"He didn't spring me?" Scott asked with a tone of confusion.

"Nope, didn't have a clue what you were on about," Mary said. "Now, where are we going?"

A quick internet search showed a private commercial airfield not too far away. Mary clicked her seatbelt into the socket and pulled away, following the directions from her smart phone. Scott was quiet as they drove, thinking about what he'd seen in the castle. He worked through his mind on how best to handle it.

"Let's see if we can do this with a little less killing and violence, shall we?"

Mary said, bringing Scott back into the moment.

"What?" Scott asked.

"A little less violence. Let's try more pleasantness and fewer murders," Mary said as they drove closer to the airfield.

Scott spotted a forklift backing down the ramp of a cargo plane as the last of the pallets were unloaded. He looked over to the building behind it and spotted an office entrance at the front.

"Over there," Scott said, pointing toward the huge hangar behind the cargo plane. Mary steadily drove over and parked the car outside.

"Now remember, less stick and more carrot," Mary insisted.

"You can try it that way if you like," Scott said.

"Okay, then I will." She walked into the office area, Scott was a couple of steps behind. The man in there, who was busily moving around parcels and boxes, moved behind the counter and looked over at the two of them.

"Hi, we need to get to Mexico, quickly. Two of us and a car if you can," Mary said with a smile.

"Got your passports?" the man asked.

"Erm, no we don't, but ..." Mary was cut short.

"Sorry, no passports no flight," the man said believing anything further was now wasting his time. He turned around and continued shuffling the boxes against the back wall.

"We can pay you a lot of money," Mary insisted, hoping to win him over.

"Still can't do it. If you haven't got your passports, you don't get a flight."

"It's an emergency, and we can make sure you get heavily compensated for your time."

"Still, no can do," the man said, shoving more boxes around.

"Let me know when you run out of carrots," Scott said with a smirk.

"Look, it really is important, and you'll probably get a reward as well as money and maybe even a medal. You'll be helping the American people." Mary was doing everything short of begging but getting nowhere. The guy grabbed a couple of boxes and walked out through the doorway at the back and into the main hangar.

"Want me to have a go?" Scott asked with a smarmy grin.

"Okay, do it your way." Mary conceded.

Scott walked through to the back room, which was only supposed to be for staff. There was a pause as he stood in the doorway for a second.

"You should have taken the money," Scott said.

* * *

Douglas had touched the helicopter down at the compound in Mexico. Napier hadn't taken long to set up his laptop in an office area inside the industrial building. The huge warehouse with an apex roof had a barred secure holding area at one end, with masses of pallet racking filling the open space in the middle and doors leading to a maze of office suites on several floors to the right. A black convertible Corvette sat near the smaller of two roller shutter doors at the rear end. There was a large dusty parking lot out the front where the helicopter sat, and a tall metal sheet perimeter fence wrapped all around the outside of the facility. Antennae and satellites dotted the roof of the large office block, which ran the length of the side of the building and stood a few stories taller than the warehouse roof.

Napier had made his way to a more refined office suite with furniture to rival that of the castle. He set up his laptop with the countdown timer displayed, then moved to a kitchen area to make himself a coffee.

"If they don't give me what I want by the deadline," Napier said to Douglas, "then I'll increase the stakes for next time. Make them ask; how many lives need to be lost before they finally give me what I want?" He was more than prepared to push the body count from ten thousand to fifty thousand if he had to make the ultimatum again. He was determined to make sure they gave in to his demands, and if that meant more people had to die, then that's what he'd do. It's not like it made a huge difference. He was intent on alleviating a huge percentage of the population from existence anyway. A few losses along the way would lighten the load when it came to the execution of the grand plan. This was only stage one.

* * *

The pilot's broken nose and bruises didn't seem to affect his flying abilities as they soared toward Mexico with the Porsche securely strapped down in the cargo hold. They'd made it to Napier's complex quicker than they expected, too. The pilot circled around.

"Can't land down there. The area's too densely populated," the pilot said.

Scott looked down and could see Napier's helicopter. The compound was way too small to land an aircraft of this size. There was a built-up area surrounding it, so touching down close wasn't an option either. They would have to land elsewhere and drive back.

"It's okay, get us over there and we'll roll the car out and drive the rest of the way," Scott said, pointing through the front window to a clearing just short of the horizon.

Within minutes they had set down and were reversing the Porsche out of the back of the body of the aircraft's hold, down the ramp, and onto the dusty Mexican road. They thanked the reluctant pilot, who was now just happy to get away from them. They drove off with haste, back toward the compound, the huge cargo plane passing them overhead shortly afterward.

Pulling in to park and out of sight as best they could remain under the circumstances, Mary shut off the engine. Leaving the Porsche parked in the shade, they walked the short distance to the compound perimeter adjacent to the street they'd parked.

The front gates were huge and locked, secured with a thick chain and padlock.

"What are you thinking?" Mary asked, seeing the look of concern on Scott's face.

"If we can't find a more vulnerable spot as we walk around the outside, then we may have to go in noisy and ram the gates," Scott said, pacing around the fence line and looking for weaknesses as they walked. "I'm not too happy about that, I'd rather try and sneak in quietly and get the upper hand."

"Yes, that worked out well last time," Mary replied sarcastically.

They carried on to the end of the fence and turned left. A short way down, Scott spotted an opportunity. A single galvanized steel, slatted pedestrian gate at the rear.

"Perfect," Scott said under his breath as he stopped to examine the sturdy gateway.

"It's locked tight. How are we possibly going to open that?" Mary asked.

"Easily," Scott replied, walking back to the car. After a quick rummage through the trunk, Scott found what he was looking for. He grabbed the scissor jack and walked back to the gate, Mary tagged along, wondering how he was going to get the gate open.

Scott placed the scissor jack on its side between two of the gate's slats, on top of the cross bar at the bottom of the gate, to which the vertical slats were bolted to. A few winds of the handle and the coach bolts holding the slats in place were under enormous tension. Not long and the slats had started to cripple under pressure from the jack.

With a few more turns of the handle and the bolts holding the slats in place finally snapped. Scott pushed the jack through, spread the slats open, and stepped through like he was walking through a gap in a pair of curtains. Mary followed, impressed with his improvization skills.

"Well, I wouldn't have thought of that," Mary said.

"That's because you've spent most of your adult life in a college and I've spent most of my adult life in a prison." Scott chuckled.

They moved quickly around the front of the building. A single wooden access door was unlocked and they slipped into the dimly lit warehouse. The first thing they noticed was the black Corvette facing the roller-shutter ready to go. A small black flight case was wedged behind the passenger seat. Mary pulled it free and opened it. Vials of nano fluid and sealed syringes filled the case. She closed it and slipped it back. They spotted Douglas moving around through the warehouse.

"You see if you can locate Napier. I'll take care of him," Scott said.

Mary nodded and moved to the right to head toward the office suites. Scott stepped out and advanced toward Douglas. He was almost upon him when his foot collided with a metal pipe he hadn't seen in the dingy warehouse. The noise startled Douglas, and he drew his pistol, spinning on the spot to face Scott.

Both of them, about thirty feet apart, pointed their pistols at each other. Arms outstretched and ready to fire.

"What you gonna do, Lomax? You ain't got no jurisdiction down here." Douglas snarled.

"I ain't got no jurisdiction anywhere," Scott replied.

It dawned on Douglas that Lomax wasn't FBI. He wasn't there to make an arrest. His finger took up first pressure, ready to squeeze the trigger.

Chapter 22

Even with the distance between them, Scott could still clearly see the moment when Douglas was lining up the shot.

Scott took a dive to his right. Firing off two shots as he went. The loud noise of the bangs filled the huge warehouse. They were more to serve as a distraction than hit the target.

Douglas's shot marginally missed Scott, skimming by and hitting the racking behind him. But a miss was a miss. That was the most important thing, in Scott's opinion, at the time. He scrambled to get up and "Off the X" as it's known. He jumped forward and turned right, then left between aisles of pallet racking. Putting angles and distance between him and Douglas until he could compose himself.

Scott moved to an area where he seemed reasonably concealed and slowly looked around some steel drums to see if he could figure out where Douglas was. He jumped back as two shots clanged into the steel drums, shortly followed by the report of gunshots, the echoing of the bangs sounding through the warehouse.

"Shit!" Scott said, moving back a touch more and in as tight as he could get behind the drums. He gave it a moment and ran back in the direction he came from. Four shots, in rapid succession, clanged at the pallet racking around him as he ran to cover yet again. The bangs of each shot filling the warehouse once again. He jumped in behind an area of racking that was stacked with wooden pallets that he could use as a shield.

The wood of the pallets splintered with two more bangs, followed by a click. That was it. This was the moment he could move. Ten rounds had been fired, and Douglas's magazine was empty. Scott ran, hoping to catch him before he could reload. He'd shoot him now while he had the chance. Scott moved around the end of the pallet in the direction the shots were fired from. He scanned as he sprinted through the warehouse, ready to shoot as soon as he saw his target. As he ran past a tall stack of pallets, Douglas swung a bar, whacking Scott's fingers and sending the gun spinning across the warehouse floor under the racking.

He looked back up in time to see Douglas swing the bar again. Jumping back the bar barely missed him. Scott stepped forward and held Douglas's arm tight, stopping him from pulling the bar back and taking another swing.

Realizing he wasn't going to break free easily, Douglas dropped and rolled backward, pulling Scott with him. Scott slammed down onto the floor behind him and rolled to his left, as Douglas managed to get up quickly and swing the bar again, hitting the floor inches from Scott's head. Scott jumped up and ran into Douglas, slamming him into the pallets, and knocking the wind out of him. Douglas dropped the bar, and Scott grabbed his shirt with both hands, swinging him around and slamming him again into the pallets on the other side.

Now was not the time to slow things down but pick things up. Scott had been in enough fights to know when you gain the upper hand, hit harder and faster so you don't lose it. Scott's first punch to Douglas's face was a solid hit on the nose. He kept his left hand on Douglas's shirt as he pummelled punch after punch into Douglas's face.

Scott let go of Douglas's shirt for one last right hook to send Douglas flying across the room and down onto the floor. Douglas landed face down and didn't get up. Scott panted to catch his breath. After a few gulps of air, he turned to look for his gun. He walked over toward the shelves it had slid under and bent down to retrieve it. It wasn't until Douglas came crashing into him that he was even aware the man had gotten up. The pair of them went flying into the stack of pallets, sending the pile toppling over.

Before Scott had the chance to move, Douglas had jumped on top of him. His legs were on either side, holding Scott's arms down, and his full body weight stopped Scott from moving. Scott watched as Douglas pulled his fist back and braced himself to take the hit. The first one smacked him right in the cheek bone. The shock of it sent a wave of pain through his skull. Before he'd even had a chance to fully acknowledge it, the second one was delivered. Smack after smack was soon accelerated as Douglas used both hands to wildly pound punch after punch into Scott's face.

If he didn't get out of this soon, he'd be done. He faced his right hand upward and made a fist. Using the floor as a platform and his forearm as a lever, he made a movement like he was curling a weight to maneuver Douglas's leg upwards and get his arm free. Scott slammed his hand into the side of Douglas's face and twisted his body to push Douglas sideways. There was just enough of a gap for Scott to break free, and he took his chance. He got onto all fours and scurried over toward the pallets. Scott searched as he scrambled away and spotted his gun. He reached out to grab it.

Douglas grabbed his foot. Scott spun around and shot Douglas in the middle of the forehead.

Douglas dropped to the floor, and Scott's head fell backward for a second, his arm lowering and resting the gun on the floor. He was just about to catch his breath when footsteps caught his attention.

"Leave the gun there and stand up!" Napier ordered as he walked toward Scott.

Scott looked to his right and saw Mary held at gunpoint in front of Napier.

"Come on, up, up!" Napier made a waving motion with his pistol.

Scott got to his feet and faced them.

"Move. That way," Napier commanded.

Scott walked and could see the secure cage they were heading to. The barred area at the end of the warehouse. The bars went about thirty feet into the air and stopped a few feet short of the apex roof. There was nothing inside the secured cage room, just a single doorway in the middle.

"In you go," Napier said.

Scott walked in with Mary a couple of steps behind. They turned around to see the cage door swing and slam shut. The lock clicks it into place, holding it securely closed. "You were so close." Napier smiled a smarmy grin and turned away, walking to the end of the warehouse.

Scott and Mary could only watch as Napier opened the shutter and started the engine of the black convertible Corvette. He pulled it out of the warehouse door and lowered the shutter down behind him.

"Well, that's not how I hoped this was going to go," Scott said. "Still, it could be worse."

"It is worse, I'm afraid," Mary said, her face filled with dread. "When I was searching the offices, Carver called to say the White House wasn't prepared to take any chances. In case we were to fail, they've scrambled a couple of fighter jets to destroy this compound. Not long now, and we'll be getting rockets fired at us from the sky."

Chapter 23

"Wow, I've never been this popular!" Scott said sarcastically. "So many people from different levels, all are trying to kill me at once. And not for the first time in my life, I'm stuck in a cage for it."

"You might be stuck in here, but I think I might be able to get out," Mary said, looking up at a gas pipe high out of reach. "I'm going to need your help, though."

Mary explained what she needed Scott to do and started the process of mentally preparing herself. Once they were both ready, Scott clasped his hands together and knelt down. Mary stepped her foot into Scott's hands and took a deep breath.

"Ready?" Scott asked.

"Ready," she replied, looking upward.

"Three, two, one, *go!*" Scott shouted as he launched himself upward, thrusting his hands up, propelling Mary into the air.

She flew gracefully upward, arms outstretching as she rose. At first, it looked like it wasn't going to happen as Mary just managed to grip onto the pipe. She swung herself back and forth, picking up momentum each time. With the third swing, she completely flipped over the pipe, fully extended, and back down. All the way around, then again. One more time, and she flipped into the air, sailing toward a metal bar containing the wiring that fed the lighting to the warehouse. It seemed so far out of her reach, but she managed to grip it and hold herself in place, swinging back and forth.

Now above the level of the bars, Scott exhaled in relief as she swung herself again, ready to leap for the last time.

She flung herself hard, up over the top of the barred internal fence and caught the top bar, controlling her landing with ease and grace.

Scott rolled his eyes and let out another deep breath of relief.

Mary pulled herself to a standing position on the top bar of the metal cell-style fence. She bent her knees and, with an adrenaline-fuelled push, jumped into a diving roll as she landed on the top shelf of the pallet racking.

Mary quickly clambered down the pallet racking on the other side of the secure bars, and ran over to the cell style door.

"Maybe I can find a key or some way to get you out," she said with a tone of desperation in her voice.

"No time. Go after Napier!" Scott ordered.

"But the jets, the missile attack!" Mary looked at Scott, her eyes filled with emotional turmoil.

"We haven't got time! Go now!" Scott shouted. He watched as Mary turned to run out of the warehouse, only slowing to pick up Scott's pistol as she went. A few more steps, and she was leaving through the pedestrian door at the opposite end.

She sprinted full speed to the Porsche and drove it hard. The only way out of town was the direction she was heading—toward the main interstate.

She rallied the Porsche through the streets in an attempt to catch up with Napier.

"Come on, Come on," she said as she raced to catch him.

She soon spotted the Corvette, closing the gap between them.

Napier spotted the car in the rearview mirror and pulled out his pistol. He stretched his arm back and aimed toward Mary. The first two shots hit the headlight and the top of the grill.

Mary panicked but kept driving. Three more shots, all of them hitting the center of the windscreen, creating three cobweb-like shapes in the shattered glass. They were mostly in the middle, so the visibility wasn't too impaired on the driver's side. Just a couple of lines ran under and over her line of vision. The loud crack of the bullets impacting the windscreen caused Mary to jump. She eased off the gas, allowing the distance between the cars to increase. Another shot took off the passenger side mirror, followed by two more that skimmed the hood. One more hit the front of the car, and she watched as Napier tossed the handgun away.

"No more bullets!" Mary said out loud. "Now's my chance." She hit the gas pedal hard, closing the gap between them again. He swerved left, and Mary followed. Right this time, and she stayed close on his tail. He made a turn to the right, narrowly missing the side wall of a building. Mary yanked the wheel right and scraped the wall with the side of the Porsche, taking out the last remaining wing mirror. The side of the car was crumpled and striped with scars running the length of the body. She hit the gas again and kept moving, steering away from the wall.

Napier raced the corvette down the narrow street, and Mary worked hard to catch up. She was gaining on him. A truck reversing out from a driveway allowed the Corvette to slip through. The bigger Porsche hammered through the gap, but as the truck continued to reverse, it hit the rear quarter of the Porsche, causing it to buck and jump to the right. Bouncing into another wall, Mary fought to regain control over the car at the high speed she was driving.

The road opened up and she saw her chance. The massive Porsche growled as she sped up alongside the Corvette and side-swiped Napier. She sent him careering off and crashing into a fence. Mary skidded to a stop and got out of the Porsche. She ran toward the crashed corvette, stopping in her tracks as two fighter jets flew overhead. She watched in horror as the first of the jets fired two missiles off. Time slowed for a moment. The missiles rocketed toward the compound then for a second, the world slowed and went silent.

Chapter 24

The silence ended, and a huge flash of explosion preceded a boom that filled the entire city. A swell of panic consumed Mary's entire body. Swirling emotions and boiling rage filled her as she marched over to Napier, pistol raised. He was in a bad, battered, and bruised way but still alive. Blood trickled from the corners of his mouth as he remained still behind the driver's seat. She held the pistol at arm's length aiming it directly at Napier's head in the most threatening way she could.

"Switch it off!" she ordered.

Napier focused on her but only smiled. His head swayed a little, and he took a breath in before he spoke.

"You're too late," Napier said. "Nothing's going to stop it now. Anyone who's been subjected to the nanofluid is going to die!"

"This nano fluid?" Mary asked as she spotted the case stashed behind the passenger seat. She opened it and extracted one of the syringes. She pierced the foil seal of one of the vials and sucked up the contents into the syringe.

"What are you doing?" Napier asked, the panic evident in his voice.

Mary jabbed the syringe, plunging it straight into his neck.

"No!" Napier shouted as she squeezed the injection into him. "Do you know what you've done?"

"Make it stop!" Mary ordered. She watched as Napier's eyes flashed backward and forward, trying to figure out how he could end up in these circumstances. She could see him trying to figure out how he could save himself, at the same time as not stopping the attack. "Make it stop now!" she shouted, pressing the pistol firmly against the temple of his head.

"Okay, okay," Napier said lifting his laptop out of the bag and opening it. There was only minutes to go and time was running out. He jabbed frantically at the keyboard. All Mary could do was watch. He typed away and eventually hit the last key. He looked up closing the laptop lid. "It's done."

Mary walked him at gun point to the Porsche, she kept catching him glimpsing back at the Corvette. She secured him using the cable ties left over from when she and Scott were at the castle. Pushing him toward the rear door of the Porsche, she watched his head again as his eyes focussed on the Corvette once more.

"Get in," she commanded, watching his eyes that were still flicking over to his battered car. She decided to see what it was that kept causing him to look back that way. She walked over to the crumpled Corvette. Nothing caught her attention at first, but when she walked to the rear, Napier's eyes widened. She lifted the trunk, and a large black heavy-duty holdall sat there tightly wedged inside. She unzipped the flap to have a look inside.

"Holy shit!" she said almost involuntarily as she observed the contents of the bag. She struggled to lift it out and hauled it over to the Porsche. She strained to lift it into the rear of the Porsche's trunk and shut the hatch. Shaking a little, she sat back in the driver's seat and looked in the rearview mirror at Napier. He sat on the back seat, defeated.

"How much?" she asked.

"Five million," Napier replied.

"Wow," Mary whispered under her breath. She started the car with Napier in the back seat, looking like a scorned child, and pulled away. She drove toward the billowing smoke rising into the air. The closer she got, the more horrific it looked. The carnage was still blazing. Flames licking the mangled structure. She pulled the car to the side of the road opposite the burning ruins of what used to be Napier's compound.

Mary stepped out of the car and walked slowly toward the roaring fire. The crackling sound as the last of the compound burned away seemed to go quiet. Her eyes welled up with tears the closer she got. She felt the heat on her face and the smoke in the air pierced the barrier holding back the tears that were swelling in her eyes. Wet lines trickled down her dry face leaving tracks as they dripped from the bottoms of her cheeks. A sudden pang of emptiness filled her, a void she wasn't even aware she had until she'd met Scott. Now she felt a hollowness at the very thought of never having him in her life again. A lump in her throat showed as she swallowed, and her heart sank.

"What the fuck d'ya do to my Porsche?"

"Scott!" Mary exclaimed as she turned around to see him standing behind her. She jumped into him, wrapping her arms and legs around him and holding him tight. She looked at his face, her expression of relief and joy obvious. "How did you get out?"

"You've got your ways, I've got mine," Scott said with a smile. "Did you stop it?"

"Yes," Mary replied through her permanently fixed smile.

"How'd ya manage to convince him to call it off?" Scott asked. Mary dropped her legs to the floor but kept her hold on Scott. She leaned back a little and looked him in the eyes.

"I injected him with his own fluid. If the attack went forward, he'd have died, too."

"Where would you learn such devious tricks?" Scott laughed.

"I wonder," Mary replied with a smile.

They walked back to the car and sat inside.

Scott glanced back at Napier.

"You think this is all over?" Napier asked, a bitter tone prominent in his voice.

"It will be when they execute you," Mary said.

"Ha, you think the American government is going to execute me? You're fools. I weaponized sound!" Napier exclaimed, pausing for long enough for his statement to sink in. "Do you know what they did at the end of World War Two with the Nazi scientists who performed cruel experiments on people? Do you think they sentenced them when they were captured? No! They were brought back to the States and given citizenship. They were employed by the government to finish their work, but now for the US instead of Germany. Just like them, they'll never want to get rid of me. They'll want to employ me. I'll be given a full pardon on the condition I work for them, even if I don't get pardoned, I'll be given leniency. A year at the most, and it'll be like this had never happened."

"He's right," Scott said as he turned toward Napier, squeezing the trigger of his pistol.

Bullets spat out of the end of the gun in quick succession, tearing through Napier's torso and riddling his body. Scott carried on shooting every round, emptying the magazine. Scott flung the empty pistol onto the back seat next to Napier. The report of the gunshots stopped, and the ringing in the ears of Mary and Scott eased.

"So you just toss the murder weapon with your prints onto the back seat next to the body?" Mary said sarcastically.

"What do you suggest?" Scott asked. "Wipe it off and tell them it was suicide?"

Mary shook her head and rolled her eyes. She started the car and pulled away.

"At least it's over now," Mary said.

Not quite, Scott thought. He wasn't about to tell Mary that, though. He didn't want to ruin the moment by telling her how they were all still in danger, but there was one more thing that needed to be taken care of before it was finally over for good. The last challenge was going to be the hardest, though.

Chapter 25

The castle in Napa Valley had been returned to its rightful owners. The amassed wealth in cryptocurrency had gone into a scheme to compensate all of Napier's victims, including Neil Frampton, who'd sworn to now devote his time and expertise to investigating methods of new medical cures and not just the creation of drugs and pills. The world seemed to be back on track toward some sort of normality. For most people, anyway. Scott still had a thread. A very delicate thread, and today was the day he was going to start pulling to see what came undone.

Flags fluttered on the bunting in the slightest of summer day breezes. The stage had been set, and the chairs behind started to fill. TV cameras from

the national and global news networks
all pointed at the stage. They had all
rehearsed the events of the forthcoming
day several times in the way guests
would for a wedding. The Secret Service
kept the area secure and White House
staff flitted from place to place getting
everything ready.

It had been a long time since
Scott had worn a suit. The jet black two-
piece suit had been tailor made and was
a material masterpiece. Twinned with a
crisp white Saville Row shirt and subtle
silvery gray silk tie in a Windsor knot,
Scott looked almost unrecognizable
from his appearance only a few days
ago. His hair was neatly trimmed, and
he was clean-shaven with a perfect
dash of Creed Aventus for a subtle yet
sumptuous fragrance.

"If only your mother could see me now," Scott whispered to himself.

"Please try and stay out of trouble today," Carver said. "Just today. Can you do that?"

"I'll do my best," Scott replied, slapping his shoulder and walking off to make the most of the complimentary drinks and nibbles. A hollow echo from his stomach reminded him he'd skipped breakfast, and the aroma of the freshly served buffet lingered in the air. One of the kitchen staff walked past with a tray full of bite-sized gourmet cuisine. The scent alone was enough to get a rumble of agreeance from his stomach and thoughts. He was standing on his tiptoes, poised to pursue the tray of nibbles making their way toward the buffet tables, when he felt a tug on the hem of his jacket. He turned on the spot and looked down to see Nathan. Smartly dressed and almost unrecognizable, Nathan stood proudly with a smile to rival Broadway.

"I've been told that I've got you to thank for getting me out," Nathan stated.

"I made the suggestion," Scott replied with a trace of a smile forming and his eyes narrowing only slightly as he held the corners of his mouth from curling up.

"Thank you, Mr. Lomax." Nathan beamed as he spoke.

"You didn't belong in there," Scott replied, the smile fading as he recalled the memories of prison. "Now that you've got a second chance, though, what are you going to do with yourself?"

"I've got a job offer," Nathan said proudly. "Right here at the White House."

"Wow. That's a good start to your newly found freedom." Scott was impressed, but thoughts of food still remained present. "Well, stay away from anything or anyone that might jeopardize that and make the most of this opportunity. They don't come too often, trust me, kid."

"I know. I have a really good chance of making a difference here. Maybe not straight away but one day."

"And I'm sure you will, kiddo. Take care." Scott gave him a couple of gentle pats on the back near his shoulder before turning to continue his quest for some kind of brunch. Thoughts of wishing the best for Nathan were overtaken by the desire for food. For a man his size, he graciously waltzed through the growing crowds, occasionally making conversation with the people he passed on his way.

Scott had the chance to mingle with and talk to the eclectic mix of people from all levels in the White House. Kitchen staff to heads of government departments. He wandered through the gardens taking in all he could, with a touch of people watching while he was at it. A large stand had been made in tribute to Gregory Kessler. Several photos of Kessler with printed pages of his accomplishments and other information stood proud among the flowers and wreaths. Scott made his way over toward it with the intention of talking to the two ladies laying more flowers at the base.

"Were you close?" Scott asked as the first of the two ladies looked up to see who'd blocked out most of the sunlight.

"I worked with him for nearly seven years," she replied.

Scott noticed that she didn't actually answer the question he'd asked. Instead, she'd given an answer that would have typically been accepted by most people. Scott wasn't like most people, though. He didn't how long she'd known him, and he didn't ask if they had worked together. He'd asked if they were close.

"He'll be missed, he was a great man," the second lady added.

"He will be missed," the first concurred. "By most, anyway."

"Who won't miss him?" Scott asked. Picking out the part of the sentence that implied most will, so some won't.

Scott chatted for a few minutes longer with the ladies before partially confirming some of his suspicions. His suspicions were the stuff nightmares were made of. Using every bit of mental strength to stay cool and keep eliciting information, he continued to talk to the two ladies.

"So, who will miss Kessler the most, do you think? Who was the closest to him?"

"Oh, definitely Gary Johnson, he was the Secret Service agent who was with him when he died. The relationship was professional, but those two were really close."

Scott talked to them for a few more minutes, asking some obscure questions about the White House that were more memorable than the questions he really wanted the answers to. This was an attempt to cover the actual questions he had wanted answers to with a smokescreen of others that seemed more specific yet unusual, maybe even a little weird.

Those would be the questions that would be more memorable, that way, if anybody asked them later what they'd talked about, they would recall the more unusual questions and skip over the more generic ones labeling them as "stuff like that."

Having as much experience as Scott did, he knew when it came to elicitation that people tend to remember the beginning and end of a conversation more so than the middle and that also people tend to remember the obscure stuff more so than the dull, run of the mill parts of a conversation.

Scott continued to do the conversation waltz through the growing crowds until he'd deliberately found himself talking to Gary Johnson, seemingly by chance. After a few minutes of chatting, Scott steered the conversation to Kessler. It wasn't long before they were talking about how he died.

"So, was he acting weird in any way on the build-up to his death?" Scott asked. He watched as Gary slowly shook his head from side to side and puffed up his cheeks. A long blowing exhale of breath ended the lip compression before Gary finally voiced his reply.

"No, not really."

"Not really?" Scott asked. He'd already established a baseline for Gary and registered his tells. The puffed-up cheeks and lip compression meant he was holding something back. This wasn't always the case for everybody, but this was definitely the case for Gary. "You look as if something's niggling you about it." Scott used his response to bait a reply out of Gary, and it worked better than he expected.

"Well, there was something," Gary stated, his face displaying he recalled the moment like a screen for his thoughts. "It was something he said just before he died." Gary paused for a moment. He squinted and tilted his head. His eyes still defocused as he replayed the memory in his mind. "He said, 'Why me?'"

"Self-pity?" Scott asked.

"No, he didn't say it in the way where he was looking for sympathy. He wasn't that kind of guy. More in the way, like he was trying to work it out in his mind. Why he had been picked out. He believed things didn't happen by chance."

"Smart guy," Scott said. "Let me ask you something. Who stood to gain the most if Kessler was taken out of the picture?"

At that moment, it was as if Gary had a long-awaited lightbulb moment. He spoke with Scott for some time with Scott building rapport as they conversed. Scott wanted to dig a little deeper yet, and Gary agreed not to act on the information until they had both got some more substantial evidence of what, at this point, in Gary's mind, was only speculation. Scott, however knew a lot more than Gary did and what he did know, was extremely disturbing.

Scott wandered into the crowd once more, casually whistling the tune of "This Old Man" as he mingled through the guests, doing all he could to keep his thoughts inside and his exterior seemingly unfazed. He slipped another glass of champagne from the tray of a passing waitress and made his way over to the buffet table. He picked up one of the many nibbles that were on offer, raised his hand ready to place it into his open mouth.

"There you are," Mary said with a playful slap to Scott's arm, sending the finger food flying to land in another section of the buffet. A disappointed look filled Scott's face as his mouth closed and his fingers snapped shut where the missing hors d'oeuvre had been propelled from. Scott had been deep in thought about the dilemma he was facing, but when he turned around, everything instantly evaporated. His mind was captivated as he looked at Mary, who'd approached him from behind and was now standing there looking at him adoringly.

She was truly beautiful. Wearing an ivory and silver lined, figure-hugging, lace dress. Complemented with strappy high heel sandals and a matching clutch, her hair styled and made up as he'd never seen her before, Scott stood there with his mouth wide open, and for that moment, there was nobody else in the world.

"Did you hand the bag into Carver?" Mary asked. Still smiling and looking like a love-struck teenager, she gave a playful yet somehow elegant bounce to her last stride toward Scott's side. She interlinked her arm with his and began to walk.

Scott snatched himself back from the daydream that had him frozen in thought, with the image of Mary looking so gorgeous paused in his mind.

"Er, yeah, I handed it back to him. It went into evidence." Scott finally replied with a bit of a stutter and was almost unaware that they had begun strolling together through the grounds of the White House. "I kept a little back for us," he said, regaining his composure and clicking back into the present moment. "You know, just a little to cover expenses and compensate us for our part."

"I can't see any reason why not." Mary agreed.

"Probably best not to tell Carver," Scott said.

"Your secret is safe with me, Mr. Lomax," Mary said, walking to the chairs on the stage that had been set up. Before Scott had even realized it, they were both sitting on folding chairs at the rear of the stage area. Sandwiched between Mary and Carver, Scott sat churning his thoughts about the recent revelations he'd unearthed.

Spokespeople all took their turn in saying their bit before the president was finally introduced and walked onto the stage to address the nation. His heart-warming speech about how a major attack was thwarted was captivating.

"Not only did we save the lives of many people, we obtained millions of dollars in digital currency that will be returned to the rightful owners, as well as three million dollars in cash that was recovered in a holdall from the proceeds of crime and handed in."

"Kept a little back for our expenses?" Mary said just loud enough for Scott to hear. A smile crossed Scott's face and his eyes creased at the corners as he looked back at Mary.

"I figured we were pretty expensive to hire," he replied quietly with a smirk looking at Mary, who was reciprocating with a cheeky smile that caused her lips to pucker like she'd heard a naughty joke that she found amusing but was trying to hide her response.

The president continued to reel off the positives from what had happened in the process of resolving the incident. He thanked the hard-working people who had all helped along the way, including Agent Carver and the director of national intelligence.

"This brings me to my next announcement. After careful consideration of the application from the director of national intelligence, I'm pleased to reveal that the current restrictions imposed upon the intelligence community are to be lifted. In light of recent events, I've come to the conclusion that sometimes good people have to do distasteful things in order to better protect the good people of this magnificent country. With that in mind, I'd like to take this opportunity to personally thank two people, in particular, starting with Mary Collins. Mary, come up here." The president made a friendly gesture with his hand.

Mary smiled as she rose from her chair at the rear of the stage. She shook hands with the president, who thanked her for her dedication before presenting her with an award. She turned in just the way they'd practiced in the rehearsal, and the president fastened the ribbon at the rear. She turned again and shook hands with the president once more. He thanked her again and as she returned to her seat next to Scott as the president continued.

"Next, I'd like to call Scott Lomax up," the president said but Scott sat there deep in thought. His mind had drifted and it wasn't until Mary subtly backhanded his leg that he came back from his trance. Scott walked forward and faced the president. "Scott, I'd like to thank you for your service to the safety of this country and the good people of America. Therefore, I grant you a full presidential pardon of all previous crimes to date." The president held out his hand.

"Including today?" Scott asked.

"Sure, why not," the president replied with a grin.

Scott reached out and grabbed the president's hand as if he'd just made a deal. The handshake concluded, Scott returned to his chair a happy man as the president wrapped up his speech.

"And now the Director of National Intelligence, Charles Driskel, would like to say a few words." The president exited as the DNI took to the stage.

"Thank you," Driskel said as the clapping and cheering from the crowd settled. They were more for the appreciation of the president than for the arrival of the DNI onto the stage, but his ego hadn't informed him of that. "I'd like to thank the president for the lifting of the sanctions, which will now allow us to work unimpeded to provide constant protection for this great nation. Scott, could you come up here once more?" Driskel asked. Scott stood and stepped forward. Driskel held out a hand. "I'd also like to thank you for your brave actions."

"I bet you would," Scott said under his breath as he gripped Driskel's hand. The handshake lingered. Driskel kept smiling as Scott grinned at him, the handshake now lasting longer than it should. The grin on Driskel's face looked even more false as he first tried to pull his hand away. Scott's grip held onto Driskel's hand and was firm. "Why don't you tell them about your part in all of this?" Scott said loud enough for everyone to hear. His hand still clamped tight and holding onto Driskel.

"What are you doing, son?" Driskel said quietly through gritted teeth doing everything he could to keep his fake smile on display through the increasing pain of Scott's tightening grip. The intensity of Scott's tight grasp increased. Driskel looked agonized.

"Why don't you tell them why you did it?" Scott said even louder this time. Squeezing Driskel's hand with a crushing vice-like grip.

"What are you on about?" Driskel was spraying saliva as he spoke, his face turning red as he fell to his knees from the waves of intense pain shooting up his arms. Mary's mouth dropped open with a gasp.

"What are you doing, Scott?" Mary whispered under her breath as she looked around in shock, only to see that everybody else seemed to be staring with a similar expression on their faces.

"Argh." Driskel winced, wriggling on his knees as Scott fiercely tensed his fist like a tightening clamp, mercilessly crushing Driskel's hand. Scott remained calm at first but got fired up as he spoke. His nose crinkled with anger at his words.

"At first, I thought it was all a bunch of little mistakes and coincidences, but too many things didn't add up. You were behind the whole thing all the time." Scott was spitting as he talked.

"What?" Driskel looked up from a kneeling position to see if he could make sense of what Scott was saying. Tears were forming in the corners of his eyes, and his face was reddening. He gave short sharp breaths, his eyes dancing with fear.

"It started when a file on Napier's desk caught my eye. Something about it just seemed out of place, like pineapple on pizza."

"What are you on about?" Driskel said with an outward burst of breath. Saliva formed at the corners of his mouth as he worked to hold his composure, hoping it would all soon end.

"It wasn't until I opened it that I realized it was you who handed everything to Napier on a plate. The CIA's nanotechnology files. The means of getting access to the satellite network and when that didn't work, you managed to get him access to the cell towers through the NSA's code. It was you who arranged delivery of the government issued spying devices found in Neil Frampton's house!" Scott shouted.

Driskel shook his head, trying to speak, but Scott cut him off. "That's how Napier knew we were coming."

Everyone got to their feet and watched as Scott spoke, making the revelations live in front of the whole world. The TV cameras zoomed in, and the crowd watched, hanging on Scott's every word. The lead Secret Service agent went to step forward and break it up, but the president held his hand out. The back of the president's hand touched the agent's chest with just enough contact to act as a physical instruction to stop and wait.

"No, just hang on a second," the president said. "I want to see where this goes."

"Of course, it was a win/win for you, wasn't it? No matter what the outcome. If I fail, then you get the restrictions lifted by saying they were to blame for the failure. The president looks bad, and you make it look like it was *his* fault that you couldn't do your job. If I succeed, you look like the hero, and you can openly say *my* success was through a lack of restrictions and enforce your point—adding further to your argument. That's why you needed me. A maniacal convict with no qualms about killing anyone that stood in my way. You knew full well the type of person I am and that I'd stop at nothing. That's why you sprung me when I got arrested by the sheriff, and that's why you deliberately used Agent Carver. A little bit of persuasion to suggest he gets me out of prison, with full White House backing."

Driskel looked around in the hopes that somebody was going to stop this madness, but everybody seemed frozen to the spot. A look of panic and dread displayed on his face as he rapidly shook his head from side to side, but Scott was far from finished.

"There was only one main player that opposed your request with the influence to sway the president's position, and that was Gregory Kessler, the Secretary of Defense. That was why he was the first to go. That was why he was singled out. That was why he was chosen to be the pawn Napier used to demonstrate his power." Scott stopped for a second and watched as the words hit home. He could see Driskel had realized he'd put it all together. Driskel's head lowered, and his physiology changed. His shoulders had dropped. He didn't even have it in him at this point to try and deny it. "But that's not the worst of it, is it? That's not the only reason you backed up this whole thing, is it?"

"No," Driskel mumbled, defeat evident in his tone.

"Tell them," Scott said, but Driskel just looked down at the floor. "Tell them!"

"With the restrictions out of the way, it meant we could operate without limitations. We could do anything and answer no one. I was going to use that power to manipulate the elections, so when the president's term ran out, I could step in as a candidate, with certainty that I was going to win," Driskel said.

"I might be a criminal, but at least I'm not a traitor," Scott said, flicking Driskel's hand away as he finally released his grip. The president gave the nod, and the officers moved in, arresting Driskel. They stood him up and cuffed him.

"This isn't over!" Driskel said out loud as he was being escorted away by the Secret Service. "The people behind me are powerful men. They won't stop. This won't change anything!" He was getting louder the farther the agents dragged him away, but Scott had lost interest. His attention had shifted to Mary, who was now casually strolling toward him with a suggestive yet proud smile. She stood directly in front of him and looked up into his eyes.

"Never a dull moment with you, is there?" Mary said. "So, now that you've got a clean slate and you're a free man, what are your intentions?"

"I'm going to go and beat the living shit out of that prison guard I promised I'd go back for!" Scott said with a frown. Mary looked up at him with one eyebrow raised. "I'm kidding." Scott laughed. "I'm going to go and spend some time with my son."

"I'm glad," Mary said, smiling.

"There is one other thing, too," Scott added. "I'm going to try my hand at chimney sweeping," Scott said with a suggestive smile.

"Then why don't you come back to my place and spend some time giving your attention to my fireplace." Mary's smile was equally suggestive.

Free sample

The Unforgien

Spy

By

Gavin Stone

Book one in the 'Spies for

Hire' Series

Chapter 1

A feeling of being watched. That's how it started.

Sandy pulled the rear door to the office closed behind her until it clicked shut. The last to leave, she hadn't realized how late it was. It seemed eerily quiet as she locked the door and slipped the keys into her pocket. An uneasy feeling of someone's presence caused the hairs on the back of her neck to stand on end.

She strode along the service road behind the block of shops and offices.

A sound—the scrape of a footstep behind her.

She looked back but saw nothing—just shadows.

She picked up her pace, silently cursing her heels and wishing she could run in them. The noise alone seemed to get louder as she clicked deeper into the narrowing alley.

There it was again. Another shuffle in the shadows.

Sure someone was there, she coughed, a futile attempt to cover her discomfort and fear. Pulse quickened, heart rate increased, she pulled her purse closer to her side and walked faster, her shoulders raised, her head lowered like a turtle. Rigid arm swings at the side of her body were quick and sharp as she hustled along.

Footsteps drew closer from behind—confirmation. There was definitely somebody there, and they were closing in. Her head felt light as fear intensified, giving her tunnel vision.

Yet, she could see the end of the road. It seemed to be taking longer to get there than it should.

Two more minutes until I get to my car.

The denial of danger in one part of her mind was battling with the growing fear in another. She was marching now. She'd gone cold, and her mouth was dry. She hadn't noticed that she'd begun to tremble. The movements of her purposeful, brisk walking covered it well.

Nearly there. She could see her car. The glow from the streetlights in the distance seemed to comfort her as she got closer.

Sandy reached into her purse, fumbling for the keys.

"Don't drop them, don't drop them," she whispered to herself. She fished them from her bag, hands shaking, then attempted to pick the right key.

The footsteps grew louder. Closer. Quicker.

"Don't look back," she mumbled.

She ran the last few yards to her car. The keys jingled as she lost her grip, dropping them on the pavement where they slid under the car.

She cursed herself as she knelt, sweeping her hand left and right under the car. Panicked, she thought of all the movies where this type of thing happened, and the killer got to the victim before they could get the key into the lock.

"Got them." She clambered to her feet and attempted to unlock the car door.

Footsteps were still behind her, getting closer. Her breathing became quicker and more shallow, the steam from her breath visible. She finally got the key in the lock, and the door unlocked.

They were right behind her now.

She dropped into the driver's seat, slamming the door shut. She quickly locked the door and looked up.

Nobody was there.

She took another deep breath. Tried to calm herself. Feeling silly but also relieved, still shaking, she inserted the key into the ignition.

A white panel van skidded to a halt behind her, blocking her car in. The side window smashed inward.

Sandy screamed.

A figure reached in and pulled up the lock.

She froze as her door was yanked open. The man pulled her out of the car, his hand wrapped around her mouth now, muffling her screams. She kicked and thrashed as he dragged her backward.

The side door of the van slid open. Sandy was shoved inside. Men inside the van held her down. She couldn't move, frozen with fear and physically restrained.

The door slid shut, then the van raced away.

The street was quiet again. Stillness in the air. The keys still swinging in the ignition of her car, the door slowly swung closed. Shattered glass peppered both the inside and the outside of her car.

Three years earlier, somewhere near the Syrian border

The black cotton pillowcase over his head let in sufficient light for Jensen to know he was still outside but provided no clue as to where he was or what was happening around him. He gulped for air, trying to get oxygen to his body. His rebel captors fired random bursts from their AKs, yelling and cheering, as they steered him roughly toward a pickup truck. He could only assume that his comrades, Marshall and James, were somewhere nearby and undergoing the same treatment. Several men grabbed him, hauling his six-foot solid, muscular frame onto the bed of the pickup truck. As he was bundled onto the deck, Jensen braced himself and pulled backward, the momentum sending him crashing into the bulkhead. The bumps and bangs confirmed that his colleagues were equally helpless and close at hand. The duct tape binding Jensen's wrists caused a sweat build-up and stung. He was forcefully held to the bulkhead as the yelling and gunfire continued.

"Breathe," he whispered, trying to calm himself with the knowledge that his captors didn't want him dead. If they did, they'd have just shot all three of them on sight. Instead, they decided to take them prisoner. This was standard procedure. The captives were made to feel disorientated and fearful in order to subdue them mentally and dash any hopes of an escape. Even though he'd been through the process many times before in training and knew each step intimately, his heart still raced. Adrenaline coursed through his body and his throat dried as he gasped for more air. The next stage of the protocol would be to display them as trophies, driving them through an angry crowd, who would happily cut their organs out with a rusty knife, given half a chance. The theory was that the fear engendered by the threat of physical violence at the hands of the rabid crowd would bring about a feeling of dependency on their captors. If successful, the hostages would feel they needed protection from the crowds, and that added strength to the strange but newly forming bond between them and their captors and outweighed the desire for escape.

The gunfire ceased as the drive to a primary holding area got underway. In line with the process, the route was, as usual, over rough terrain and followed an obscure trail to confuse the captives' sense of direction. A dust cloud billowed behind the two-truck convoy as it sped across the arid landscape, the heat from the sun causing the pillowcase to stick to Jensen's face uncomfortably. Their weapons, of course, had been confiscated upon their capture, with the day sacks following shortly afterward. Now the blindfolded Jensen felt tugs at his wrist and realized his watch was about to be a souvenir. After peeling the duct tape back from the watch, the rebel guard also decided he wanted the personalized braided Paracord bracelet, too. An argument in Arabic ensued as another of the rebels rummaged through Jensen's pockets to see what he could find. Jensen's boots caught the second man's attention and ignoring the long zipper that ran the length of the inside of the boot, which would have made the whole task a lot easier, the idiot unlaced and tugged hard to get them off.

All three of them lay stock still, stripped down to just jeans, T-shirts, and socks. None of them tried to communicate for fear of getting the business end of a rifle butt impolitely, telling them to be quiet.

Unbeknown to the hooded hostages, the trucks pulled into what appeared to be an industrial area with a large warehouse and scattered outbuildings, which were slightly sheltered by a cinderblock perimeter wall.

The yelling started again as the three men were dragged into the warehouse. All three were shouted at in Arabic as they were shoved and pulled, not knowing where they were being taken. Each of them tried to keep their footing as they were forced along a corridor and into a dim room. A steel barred door was slammed shut behind them as they were shoved to the floor. Jensen was conscious of the sound of a padlock snapping shut and the footsteps of their new guard as he retreated down the corridor.

Jensen pulled the damp pillowcase off his head and let his eyes adjust to the faint light from the small, barred window. The air was humid and stale. The room, now coming into focus, allowed him to see the other two pulling the covers from their heads and the figure of a more mature but equally disheveled-looking man sitting on a chair, hands cuffed behind his back. The stench of stagnant sewage and body sweat filled the air as all three men scanned the room. The rotten plaster was falling off the walls, and the paint only seemed to stay for lack of better places to go. The concrete floor was peppered with litter and blood splashes. The man on the chair looked bemused at the reactions of the threesome.

"You took your time!" he shouted.

"Love what you've done with the place, sir!" Jensen chirped in a cheerful English accent as he got up to look for a right angle in the wall's brickwork. At the barred window, there was a perfect corner for his purpose. He rubbed his wrists up and down to fray the duct tape and free his hands. "I'm trained for this," Jensen muttered to himself.

"Get me out of here," their newly reunited friend groaned. Harrison was Marshall's former department head from when Marshall came over from the

States to work for the Brits. Marshall may have been working as a contractor now, but Harrison still commanded the kind of respect he expected when working for him in the past. All three of them worked freelance and had been hired to complete a Target Acquisition job by a PMC. Either way, Marshall still addressed Harrison as "sir" and still kept a good level of professional conduct. A good level for Marshall anyway.

"Yes, sir." Marshall stood and pulled down his jeans.

"Gonna ask Harrison to do you a favor first?" James asked in jest, his American accent somewhat stronger than Marshall's

"Oh, please, I'm not that desperate!" Marshall dug into his groin to peel off a strip of tape. The banter between them had become second nature and was how Jensen and Marshall took the edge off serious situations. James had occasionally worked with them in the past, but it didn't take him long to get into the same mode of thought. Marshall finished peeling the tape away, securing a button compass and a plastic handcuff key stuck to its underside.

The one area rarely checked on captives is the bridge between a man's genitals and his anus. In almost every country in the world and even amongst the most hardened of soldiers, it's a place frequently overlooked as not many men want to go through the invasive procedure of checking there and feel extremely uncomfortable doing so.

With this knowledge, the three-man team had all smuggled in a few separate bits of an Escape and Evasion kit. Marshall freed Harrison while Jensen retrieved a ceramic razor blade concealed in the same fashion.

It's amazing what you can do with a bit of skin-colored sniper tape, he thought.

***

Tension grew as everyone held their positions after they'd got into place. This was the pivotal part of the plan. If this part went wrong, it would make future escape attempts infinitely harder. Jensen silently prayed, controlling his breathing, poised to take action.

Harrison lay on the floor with James and Marshall kneeling beside him.

With a deep intake of breath, Jensen shouted to get the guard's attention. Footsteps clapped along the corridor until the guard was in sight. He ran to the caged door, peering through the bars.

Inside, the chair had toppled to the floor, and one of his prisoners appeared to be suffering some sort of seizure. With a sense of urgency, he opened the cell door and rushed inside toward Harrison. He prodded James with the barrel of his weapon and motioned for both men to move aside, failing to notice that the duct tape no longer bound their hands.

As he knelt to examine the stricken prisoner, Jensen approached from behind. Before the guard was aware of his presence, Jensen pulled the guard's forehead back with his left hand and reached around the front of him with his right hand. He sliced the man's throat with the ceramic razor and, stepping back, lay the guard down slowly onto the floor.

Tradecraft: *The trick is to cut straight, continuing at the same depth from one side to the other, and not to move outward with the shape of the neck. Moving along the natural shape of the neckline will result in only slicing the skin. The damage will be horrendous, but death is not inevitable and will take much longer. Thus giving the subject the chance to react or retaliate in a desperate attempt of defense. Starting from one side and cutting straight across at the same depth will result in the blade going deeper into the curve of the neck. Ultimately cutting the windpipe, muscles, and arteries. Death is much quicker, and the chance of retaliation much lower.*

Blood pumped out over Harrison as the guard grabbed at his throat. Neck scarf soaked, panic in his eyes, the guard struggled as he grasped the front of his neck. There was a gargling noise as he lay there spitting and coughing. Blood seeped through his fingers as it bubbled in his futile attempts to cling to life. His final breaths became shallower as Jensen looked into his eyes. The pupils dilated, then nothing. Like a light switching off, the life was drained from him, the only remaining motion the expanding pool of blood.

The three of them rapidly distributed the guard's possessions between them. It was decided that James would have the boots, as he was a size nine. Because he got the boots, Marshall and Jensen got the toys. Marshall performed the standard checks on his new AK47, and Jensen pulled back the top slide of the Colt 1911.

"Can you get me out of here now?" Harrison grumbled impatiently.

"Yes, sir," Jensen replied. "Marshall will be running point, you stay between James and me, and I'll be at the rear."

"Okay, just get on with it." Anxiety laced Harrison's voice.

It seemed to Jensen that the operation was going to plan—so far at least. Knowing they'd be out-gunned and outnumbered, the odds seriously stacked against them, the team had previously set up an observation post to assess the situation. Having identified where their high-priority target was being held, they concluded that the extraction would be much easier if they got themselves captured and driven straight through the front door rather than attempt a pre-dawn raid with all guns blazing. After all, it would be much quicker to shoot your way out if you didn't have to shoot your way in first. It was a risky plan at best, but there wasn't much else in the form of options. Not to mention they weren't one hundred percent sure exactly which part of the compound their target was actually in. They would have had to use up more time and ammunition to find him, lowering the chances of success even more. However, the uncertainty of the situation required that they act quickly before their target was moved to another location. Acquiring the target was only half of the equation, and of necessity, the exit strategy was somewhat crude. Any hope of success required planning. For this, James had cached some useful kits and weapons in various strategic locations around the perimeter wall.

Marshall exited the room into the corridor holding his new AK at the ready. Jensen moved out and over to the other side of the corridor, pistol in hand. Their socks dampened their footsteps on the stone floor, allowing them to move quickly and quietly as they inched along.

They neared the end of the corridor that opened to the right into a large guard room. One man sat on a shabby sofa in the middle of the floor, watching an outdated television. An AK was propped beside him.

Controlling his breathing, Jensen moved as slowly as he could. His socks left momentary moisture marks on the floor with each step. Not having his boots on might have given him a slight feeling of vulnerability, but it definitely gave him a tactical advantage. Aware of Marshall's movements to his left, he inched closer.

Three other doors on the other side of the room allowed access, but only one was open. The open one revealed sunlight from the outside courtyard. Jensen saw Harrison and James making their way silently up the corridor in his peripheral vision. He looked back at the guard as he eased forward.

When Marshall gave a signal to Jensen, he moved into the room. His movements were slight to avoid the noise of his clothes rubbing, the tension of the task increasing the closer he got to the guard.

Marshall eased stealthily to the left, AK raised, ready to give the guard the good news if it went noisy. The guard was deeply engrossed in whatever TV show he was watching.

Jensen eased up behind the guard until he was only inches away. He drew back his fist and snapped forward with a rapid strike to the back of the guard's head. The potentially deadly blow knocked him out instantly while Jensen swooped in and swiftly scooped up the AK47 that sat beside the tumbling guard.

Tradecraft: *The trick is to punch the back of the head at the soft spot where the base of the skull meets the neck. Hitting the bottom right corner with the punch aimed diagonally up in the direction of the left eye has a devastating effect. Equally hitting the bottom left corner with a punch aimed diagonally up toward the right eye has the same result. The blow will incapacitate; a single blow can even prove fatal. The strike will usually knock a person unconscious but can kill if enough force is used.*

James came into the room with Harrison, and Jensen handed him the pistol while making the necessary checks on the AK. Marshall moved to cover the doors in case anyone came through after hearing the thud of the guard hitting the floor, but before he was halfway there, the door on the left rattled.

Their window of relief was only momentary.

The door burst open. Two rebels stormed into the room, brandishing AKs and yelling in Arabic.

Jensen watched as James raised the pistol with his right hand, shoving Harrison behind him and into the corridor with his left hand.

One rebel let out a burst of shots. Jensen dove to the floor, returning fire. A burst of three rounds pierced straight through the rebel to the left. Marshall fired at the one on the right. A tight group of holes had gone through the center of his chest and through the wall behind him, too. Both men dropped to the floor. Without thinking, Jensen's training kicked in. He rushed forward and turned the first body over, kicking the man's weapon toward the corridor. James didn't need to wait for an invite. He snatched it up and handed the pistol to Harrison.

Moving quickly, Jensen repeated the procedure, ejecting the magazine from the AK and stuffing it into his back pocket. Before they had time to move, shouting was heard from the courtyard.

"Shit! We have to get out of here before this becomes a gang fuck!" Marshall moved toward the open door, weapon raised. The gate was about a hundred meters away, with only a couple of trucks for cover. "I'll take James and run for the trucks. You lay down suppressing fire as we move out, and then we'll return the favor as you join us."

Marshall waved in a calling motion at James as he leaned against the doorframe, preparing himself for the run. "Three, two, one, go!"

Letting off a couple of short bursts from his rifle, Marshall ran toward the trucks, sand being kicked up by his socks as he ran, James a second behind him.

Jensen sprang into the doorway. Spraying bursts of fire in the direction of the noise. Rebels fired from crevices around the compound. The familiar cracks of 7.62 rounds sounded all around him.

Jensen continued with his bursts of suppressing fire randomly, then paused and looked over to see if Marshall and James had made it to the cover of the engine blocks of the trucks. A crack of shots hit the doorway and caused him to jump backward. The bullets splintered the wood, peppering plaster and powder into the air. Jensen dropped farther back inside for cover.

His heart raced, and sweat covered his face. Adrenaline surged through him as he took a deep breath again.

Another burst of shots cracked into the walls around the doorway. A few pierced through the guard room and hit the wall behind him. The TV screen shattered.

Jensen ran over and shoved the chair at the two doors that allowed entry to the room, slamming one shut with the action. Then he propped the chair in place and shoved a table in front to stop it from sliding back, blocking both doors. At least no one would get in through either of those doors in a rush.

Marshall and James had gotten into position and were returning fire.

It was now or never.

Jensen grabbed Harrison by the scruff of the neck and ran out of the doorway. Bursts of fire hit the floor around them. He gave it all he had, sprinting toward the trucks, practically dragging Harrison behind him.

Marshall and James were firing at anything that moved, but the number of rebels were increasing. The return fire was becoming more intense. Jensen tucked in as rapidly as he could behind the cover of the trucks. His chest heaved as he gasped to catch a breath.

There wasn't enough time or ammunition for another two-part run. They'd all have to make a dash for the gate together. Being nearly out of ammo wouldn't stop them from shooting as they went, with probably just enough to get them to the other side of the gate that marked the only opening in the cinderblock walls.

They all knew the score. Nobody said anything. They all knew what each other was thinking. A look was all it took.

In unison, all four of them broke cover for the gate.

Bullets thudded into the ground around them as they ran. Their small target was about twenty meters away, but it took ages to get there. They all fired off shots as they ran toward the gate with everything they had.

Nearly there—almost through.

Marshall had his weapon about waist as a rebel came from the other side of the gate just as Marshall got there.

Time stopped as the rebel stood there, weapon aimed at Marshall.

Marshall had his aimed at the rebel as he continued to run.

The cracks of weapons firing around them seemed to dampen. Everyone was moving but somehow still seemed frozen to the spot.

Marshall's weapon spit several bullets and the rebel dropped as Marshall ran into him and through the gate. Then he checked himself. "Phew! No new holes!" He gulped for air and tried to catch his breath as relief flooded through him.

Jensen kneeled to grab the magazine from the rebel's rifle, relieved his friend was okay. His leg muscles felt like they were on fire while sprinting in the heat, and his pulse throbbed away as he tried to catch his breath. Two more mags were in an ammo pouch on the rebel's belt. He distributed them not a moment too soon. The next wave of rebels rounded the corner of the cinderblock wall. Marshall and James spun on the spot to fire toward them.

Another group was heading toward the gate from the inside. Jensen fired into the compound, taking down three of the rebel guards. The small group on the outside had been neutralized. It was time to move out.

As the four ran from the area toward their cache, they scored another Kalashnikov and an antique, NATO-issue, Browning HP from a couple of rebels on the wrong end of a bad day. With all four now armed, they were marginally better equipped to shoot their way out to the exfil point. It was fortunate that the compound had proved only lightly guarded, with most of the rebels away, no doubt engaged in some nefarious enterprise.

But in the ensuing fire-fight, at least ten more rebels got slotted as the results of the group's exit strategy. The return fire from the compound continued sporadically as they battled their way out of the area, with a few rebel troops in close pursuit. The group reached one of James's hidden caches and punched out a get-me-home signal on a sat phone buried there, with a couple of loaded Gen4 Glock 17s and some extra and much-needed ammunition.

They were all close to exhausted and gasping for breath as they held their position at the exfil point for the chopper. Time ticked away, and ammo was limited. They did everything they could to hold down their position. Fueled on adrenaline, pulses racing, they returned as much fire as they dared while still trying to use the ammunition sparingly.

There was no sign of the helicopter and no way they could hold their position for long. Marshall was beginning to fear the worst. Jensen had already concluded that this might be their last stand. How the hell could they get out of this one if the chopper didn't show up?

Rebels were closing in, and their ammo was running out.

***

The sounds of the rotor blades coming in from above, accompanied by the roar of the chopper's engine, filled Jensen with hope. Marshall fired his last few rounds off from his AK before switching to his sidearm, then looked up, still firing as the helicopter descended. The downdraft pounding the floor kicked up a wall of sand around them. The smell of spent fuel filled the air, and they could feel the heat from the helicopter's engine being pushed by the rotor's downdraft. Jensen spent his last couple of rounds firing toward the enemy as the chopper closed in.

The helicopter gunner rattled away a "mass of brass" to keep the rebels at bay, and not a moment too soon as the team was pretty much out of ammo. While Jensen and Marshall gave the older Harrison a boost, James turned to lay down more covering fire with his last few rounds. With all the noise and commotion, nobody noticed he'd taken a hit until he dropped his weapon and toppled face down in the sand. Jensen and Marshall grabbed an arm and unceremoniously hauled him aboard the chopper as it began to rise.

Marshall and Jensen knelt on either side of James. Only his top half was moving, his chest heaving rapidly up and down and his head going slightly side to side with eyes wide as he looked around in desperation. Marshall used his knife to cut away the clothing from the wound. Jensen grabbed Kwik Clot from the onboard trauma pack as they battled to save James's life.

"Hold on, pal," Marshall yelled over the deafening roar of the engine as the chopper gained altitude. The pleading look in his eyes spoke volumes to Jensen, who was doing all he could. James's breathing became increasingly rapid and more shallow. Then the quick succession of shallow breaths slowed until the life drained from his eyes.

Jensen watched as yet again he witnessed the life of another human being extinguished. Marshall attempted CPR, but Jensen knew that their companion was gone. He brushed his fingers over James's face closing his eyes. Nobody spoke further.

All three men buckled themselves into their seats and looked down at their lost companion. The ride in the helicopter seemed to take forever as Jensen sat with sobering thoughts of mortality. James's leg moved from side to side under the motion of the rotor blades, one recently liberated boot swaying back and forth. You could almost think he was merely catching some well-deserved sleep if not for the hole in his torso covered in blood.

The dead guard's boots dragged Jensen's mind back to the haunting look in the eyes of the man as he died. Jensen spared no thought for the others he had killed in the fire-fight, but when you cut a man's throat and look into his eyes, it becomes personal. That pitiful look, screaming for help before the light was extinguished and the life drained away, was exactly the same as that in the eyes of his friend. James had dedicated his life to working in the shadows of a covert world and would now be nothing other than a black star, a name in a book, and another wall decoration. His accomplishments were never recognized, and his service was never rewarded. This was exactly the type of stuff he wanted to keep his baby girl away from.

Chapter 2

The cuckoo clock on the wall would normally have been alerting the world that it was nine o'clock in the evening, but a few weeks after bringing it home, the novelty of its call had worn off, and it was decided to leave it in silent mode. The wooden contraption looked somewhat incongruous amongst the modern interior and designer furnishings, but it was a souvenir of a trip to Switzerland before they'd actually moved into the house and decided upon the décor. Most of the pictures and canvases in the room were portraits of Jensen and his wife MJ or photos of their precious baby girl Elena, all except one.

A picture in a silver frame of his late comrade, James, out of his combat gear, standing beside MJ in front of Big Ben.

Jensen relaxed on the couch in the dimly lit room, nursing a large glass of Russian vodka. He placed his glass on the coffee table, showing his replacement paracord bracelet. A carbon copy of the one he'd lost. MJ was lying across him in a blue satin negligee with an oversized but well-deserved glass of white wine, her long blond hair still slightly damp from her long soak in the bath. With Elena finally asleep, the two of them were getting cozy, ready for a little Netflix and chill. As any full-time parent of a toddler will tell you, "Netflix and chill" translates to "sit and dribble" until you drag your sorry ass off to bed and sleep. Elena was the cutest little girl they could ever ask for, Jensen thought, but she was also one hell of an effective contraceptive. A subtle smirk and mischievous glint in MJ's big blue eyes indicated to Jensen that she was silently teasing him.

"What?" Jensen asked in profane innocence.

"Nothing," MJ replied innocently as she unbuttoned Jensen's shirt. "I was just thinking about the day we met."

"And thinking what might have happened if we hadn't?" Jensen asked. "You'd probably have married that accountant. What's his name? Fred? Ted?"

"It was Jed."

"Whatever. A dutiful housewife meeting the other moms for lunch and to talk plastic surgeons."

"Would not." MJ gave him a

playful slap across the chest. "I'd have retrained, taken that law degree I was thinking about and been fast-tracked to partner."

"But instead, you're half a world away, collapsed on the sofa on top of your stay-at-home husband after a long day in the world of corporate recruitment."

"And I wouldn't have it any other way," she said as she undid another button of Jensen's shirt and slipped her soft hand through the gap, probing the rock-hard torso. "You remember the barbecue?"

"Are you kidding me?" Jensen replied. "I couldn't stop drooling, and it wasn't the steaks." He'd always be grateful that six years earlier, he'd accepted an assignment as an "off the books" contractor from an acquaintance named Max, who was working from a C.I.A. outpost in a particularly nasty part of the world. When the contract was satisfactorily concluded, Max had invited him to stay in California for a while.

"I think it was your accent," MJ said. "You looked okay, but when you opened your mouth …"

"My accent? Maybe I shouldn't have brought my gorgeous American missus back to merry old England where it's full of blokes with English accents."

"Maybe it's a little more than the accent. Burgess Hill isn't exactly teeming with charming trained killers."

"Perhaps not the most useful skill for a quiet life in the commuter belt," he said.

"Do you miss it?" she asked, pulling her head back slightly and displaying genuine concern in her eyes.

"We've been through this," he said after a long inward breath. "It's not just about me anymore. It's not even about you and me. I'm not flying around the world leaving you looking after Elena on your own, wondering if I'm coming back." He couldn't help himself looking at the photograph of James and MJ on the side.

The turning point had come the evening when MJ joyfully announced that the "perfect two" were soon to become three. Over the next few months, Jensen unconsciously reduced his workload, sidestepping contracts as MJ's pregnancy progressed. Eventually, he became unavailable and took a job working locally in the security industry as a temporary measure. It meant he could be working while staying close to home for when the baby was born. After Elena made her appearance, Jensen quit the security work and went back to what he knew best, and for what he had been so intensively trained, taking on a few short-term contracts. At first, the familiarity of being back on the job was invigorating after the dull routine of security work. But somehow, it was different now.

MJ turned his head back from the photograph and kissed him. "When I was pregnant, and you started doing that local security stuff, you were so bored. I hated it."

"Not as much as me," Jensen said.

"I know you had to get back to work properly after, but I am glad you've stopped. I didn't think you could be any more amazing when I first saw you at that barbecue, but you're an amazing stay-at-home dad."

"You think?" Jensen took a glug of his vodka.

"Yes, I do think." MJ finished her white wine and set the glass on the coffee table. "And I also think it's time you had your reward."

Jensen put his glass down without finishing it and let MJ's lips meet his again.

Then the doorbell rang.

"At this time?" MJ muttered.

"I'll go." Jensen re-buttoned his shirt as he made his way out of the living room toward the front door, shouting "Coming!" to their mystery visitor who had by now rung the bell three times.

Jensen opened the door and Marshall shoved his way inside. "We need to talk. Now!"

Jensen had no idea why Marshall was so rattled. Whatever it was had to be important for him to come at this time of night. He skipped the pleasantries and ushered Marshall in.

The three of them gathered around the dining table as Marshall played a video on his phone. It showed Sandy, Marshall's recently estranged ex-girlfriend, sitting in a chair with tape over her mouth; she looked scared witless. She was obviously bound to the chair, but the restraints couldn't be seen. Her forehead was covered in sweat, her hair soaked, and she was breathing heavily. Fear showed in her eyes as she screamed, the muffled noise held in by the tape. Her head was jerked back violently, and an arm came around her neck, the rest of the person out of view. Her attempts to scream increased, and the fear in her eyes peaked as the hand revealed a ceramic razor. The skin was pierced, the razor dug in deep, and the cut was deliberate and slow. Sandy obviously felt every second of it, every ounce of pain displayed in her eyes. The struggle continued as panic rose to the surface. She was terrified. She knew this was the end. Finally, her head dropped forward, and the tension stopped. She was gone. Blood poured down the front of her lifeless body, then the video stopped abruptly.

The battle-hardened Marshall put on a brave face, but Jensen knew he was hurting and felt his pain. MJ's hands covered her mouth, as she sat in shock at what she'd just seen.

Tears in the corners of his eyes threatened to flow, but Marshall held them back.

"Where's it from?" Jensen asked, watching Marshall, who was still struggling to maintain his composure.

"I don't know. It was sent to my phone earlier. No demands, no speech, nothing."

"Does anyone else know?" Jensen asked. Subconsciously he was aware of a shift in MJ's posture, but it didn't alert him just yet. He dismissed it as her feeling uneasy after viewing such horrific footage.

"I'm going in to report it, but I wanted to show you first. Just in case … you know." Marshall looked pointedly at MJ, then back at Jensen.

"Do you want me to come with you?" Jensen was concerned for his colleague's state of mind, but Marshall seemed to have regained a measure of self-control.

"No, I'll be fine. Just watch your six."

Jensen stood and clasped his friend's shoulder. "You too, mate. Let me know how it goes, and if you need me for anything, I'm here."

Marshall left without another word.

Jensen closed the door behind him and downed his vodka before pouring another large one. He sat at the dining table opposite MJ, who had remained silent since watching the video. Something didn't seem right.

"Are you okay?" he asked.

Of course, he knew it was a futile question, but he had a feeling that something was off and wanted to try and work out what it was. "Is it Sandy?"

"Yes. Well, no, I just feel for Marshall is all," she said. "Seeing her killed that way." MJ sat facing him with her words, belying what her body was telling him.

Tradecraft: *TSA agents working at the airport are trained to watch a person's feet as they stand at passport control. If they stand straight, everything is usually okay. Still, if their body is straight and their feet are facing the exit, it's a sign of their being extremely uncomfortable and wanting to get away as quickly as possible.*

MJ's feet were pointed toward the door.

"Was it something you saw in the video?" He kept his voice soft, gentle.

MJ's hand went up and twiddled with her Tiffany necklace, a first-anniversary present that Jensen had bought for her when they were visiting America. Jensen recognized the discomfort in her body language; he was sure she'd seen something.

"No, I told you. I'm just upset about what happened." He observed the position of her arms, covering particular areas, one arm flat on the table shielding her torso, the other fiddling with the necklace in front of her throat. It was the limbic brain's way of protecting herself. Subconsciously she was guarding her throat and vital organs, a reaction a person inadvertently performed in times of discomfort or deceit.

"What was it? What did you see?" he pushed.

"How do you do this to me? How do you always know what I'm thinking?" she asked.

"Come on, MJ, it's important." he said.

"I know who was in the video. I know who cut her throat." Her voice wavered as she spoke. Her face displayed fear and confusion.

"Who? Who was it?" he asked. "How do you know them?"

She seemed to be weighing her options, working out what to say and do. MJ had turned her body slightly away from Jensen, her feet now fully pointing toward the door. She displayed signs of being cold and hugged her shoulders.

Jensen was becoming tense. "Come on, MJ, who was in the video?"

His voice had raised, and she met his gaze. Her hands were now spread as she leaned onto the table.

"YOU!" she yelled. "It was you!"